INQUIRIES & ADVERTISING

Address: Suite 22, 509 Commissioners Road West, London, Ontario, N6J 1Y5
Advertising: Email info@mysterymagazine.ca
Editor: Kerry Carter **Publisher:** Chuck Carter **Cover Artist:** Robin Grenville Evans
Submissions: https://mysterymagazine.ca/submit.asp

GONE TO WEAVE BY STEAM

Kelsey Hutton

"What ... what is it?" Alice stammered out, wiping sweat off her forehead with a soot-streaked forearm.

She reluctantly pulled her attention away from the roasting screen, where the haunch of venison wrapped in bacon crackled and spit in the fireplace. The kitchen was quieter than it usually was, with so many of the servants away. But the meat juices were dripping, the soup simmering, and the jellies setting. It was already late afternoon, and even with the large kitchen windows, Alice could tell by the fading light it was almost time for the first course to be served. It was the worst possible time for Lady Winthrope to come clopping into the kitchens to show off ... what, exactly?

Whatever it was, it wasn't for eating. Alice could smell the rot from here, even over the venison.

Through the swinging doors to the scullery, Sally had stopped scrubbing the family's china in the copper sink to crane forward, trying to catch a look. "Don't let your elbows get dry," Alice called loudly over Lady Winthrope's shoulder. Sally rocked back on her heels and grinned, but dutifully sloshed her boiled arms back into the greasy water.

The mistress held her prize out to Alice regardless, and she gingerly examined it without touching. It was roughly the size of a small melon, with what looked like brown spiky scales. Each of the scales tufted into a dry husky tip curled upwards. At its top, like a lady's hair piled high, were thick curly green fronds. Even Lady Winthrope held it carefully to avoid touching the pale green mold creeping lightly up one side.

"It's called a 'pineapple,' it is from *South America*, and it is a great honour that the Lady Ryder brought it for us," Lady Winthrope said, though her face could not muster up the same enthusiasm as her words. Her eyebrows crinkled doubtfully.

Alice swallowed back a sigh. The Winthropes never could resist anything that would make them seem a higher station than they really were. "It is ... moldy, my lady," Alice said slowly, as if pointing out that fire was hot. "To eat it would risk ruining dinner."

Lady Winthrope opened and closed her mouth, eyes wide, imploring Alice to find a solution. Like a child with hands too full of stolen biscuits to eat the pudding served to her.

Alice glanced behind Lady Winthrope at the shallow pot with the chestnuts in it. She couldn't see them from here, but she could smell them, which meant they needed to come off the fire soon.

All this was taking too much *time*.

"How about we use it as a centerpiece?" Alice offered.

"A centerpiece, yes, thank you, Mrs. Wade!" Lady Winthrope exclaimed in relief. Alice took the prickly thing and made room for it on the kitchen table. This jolted several fruit flies out of their hiding spots, and Alice held back from swatting them away while the mistress was still here. Lady Winthrope glanced behind her at Sally's back, suddenly conscious of her audience. "Just be sure to turn the moldy side underneath, and that no one cuts into it," she whispered. "I'll foist it off on Mrs. Beckett at the end of the evening. She's to have a dinner-party next week."

Lady Winthrope turned to go, then stopped mid-way. "Oh, one last thing," she said, as if this had just occurred to her, and Alice's stomach clenched. She hadn't been in her position long—apparently Lady Winthrope had a reputation for churning through cooks—but it only took a few weeks to learn the mistress would gladly talk her way around any subject under the sun before approaching a quarrelsome subject outright. This must be the mistress's main reason for coming downstairs all along.

The hour-bell chimed distantly and Alice had to squeeze her fingers into fists to suppress her impatience. She quickly turned to call for Sally, but she was already rescuing the chestnuts. The good girl started mashing them for the soup. "Yes, my lady?" Alice said tightly, and hoped desperately it wasn't about Alice's request for leave after dinner that evening.

"Yes, well ... the Lady Ryder has done us another great honour. She, well, she brought her husband the Home Secretary and her three daughters to join the Society tonight. Surely four more mouths won't make that much of a difference?"

Four more mouths! They would need two more goose pies, four more heads of celery boiled for the salad, another dozen egg balls rolled for the soup. ... And of course, the extra time it would take to polish the cutlery once the dinner was finally over.

At this rate, it would be hours after sunset before Alice could reasonably leave the house.

But she had taken too long to answer. The quiet had grown heavy, with only the blunt sounds of Sally breaking open the chestnuts with the back of her knife to break the silence.

Into that silence, the Lady Winthrope repeated, "That will be fine, will it not?" with a voice steeled against complaint.

"Of course, my lady," Alice said.

"Your pyramid is crooked." Alice stood back behind the large wooden table, all flour and grease wiped away, and let Sally fix the dessert while she caught her breath. "Your base is the right size though. There should be just enough marzipan to make it to the top."

Sally beamed and Alice couldn't help but feel more than a twinge of pride. But she hadn't heard the last hour's bell, what with the rush to plate the venison around that dratted fruit, so she wasn't sure of the time. That pineapple or whatever it was had a crack along the bottom, and refused to sit evenly on the tray. Alice's best hope for making her appointment was that the slight tinge of mold in the air would discourage the Ladies' Society from lingering over their tea and brandy.

"There!" Sally breathed a sigh of relief, then quickly wiped off her hands before getting ready to take the last tray up. Mrs. Winthrope was terribly disappointed that their only footman had given his leave before it was her turn to host the latest party of the Ladies' Society for the Education and Employment of the Female Poor, and with the housekeeper tending to her sick sister, it was all hands on deck. But Sally didn't clean up too poorly, once you wiped off the flour. And it was only ladies, anyway, as the master of the house was away on business. Or at least, the ladies and the Home Secretary.

"And only half-past eight!" Sally crowed. Alice's heart skipped a beat. That girl. She must have been counting the bells for her all along. "Is it too late to see your son, Mrs. Wade?"

Alice's eyes prickled hot. "Not at all," she said, then cleared her throat. "I should just catch him before his ship sets sail."

"I know it's been two years since the press gang caught him," Sally continued as she carefully picked up the tray. "It would be terribly unfair if you missed him on the mistress's account—"

"Hush—" Alice cut in.

"—no matter what Mrs. Beeton and her *Book of Household Management* has to stay about it." Sally pinched her mouth up and stuck her nose up in the air. *"A lady's tongue, while firm, is the law of kindness,"* she mock-quoted from Lady Winthrope's bible. *"She looketh well to the ways of her household, without once tolerating idleness or insubordination."*

"Quiet, you, before the mistress comes down here to investigate where her dessert made off to!" Alice swotted the back of the girl's head, but gently, and let herself laugh. "Now get!"

Sally flounced off, her voice trailing behind her as she turned the corner. *"A place for everything, and everything in its place ..."*

Then a shrill scream sounded from upstairs.

"Mrs. Wade?" Sally asked uncertainly.

Then another scream, and more shouts.

"What on earth?" Alice stood behind Sally, both of them peering up the steep stairwell, but the candlelight from upstairs only dimly illuminated the way. Alice's heart thundered in her chest, so loud she could hear it. Sally was frozen, a few steps up, waiting for what seemed like an age. Then Alice realized it wasn't her heart pounding out loud, but footsteps racing down to find them.

"YOU!"

It took a moment for Alice to put a face to the pointing finger. But there was Lady Ryder, Lady Winthrope's guest of honour, a buxom woman with a set of shoulders that could drag a cart. Behind her were three honey-haired girls, presumably her daughters—the oldest perhaps one-and-twenty, the next a year or two younger, peering curiously into the dark kitchen, followed by a fey young girl of eight or nine biting her thumb. Then there was pinch-faced Mrs. Beckett, who always pointed out the water spots on spoons, and Mrs. Lowry, who had a face full of freckles. It was bad enough her skin stayed tanned a shade darker than a lady's strictly should, even in the winter. She also spoke openly of her husband's mistresses—so that she wasn't the only one in the room not in the know. Bringing up the rear, her stringy neck bobbing to see past the women in front of her, was a terribly anxious Lady Winthrope.

"YOU!" the shrill voice sounded again, and Alice realized the Lady Ryder was shaking something heavy and spewing droplets of juice in one hand. With the other, she pointed directly at—

—Sally.

"YOU DID THIS!" the woman shrieked again, and thrust the yellow thing at Sally's feet. The girl stumbled backwards, and the carefully crafted pyramid of marzipan tipped, then scattered almond paste and powdered sugar all over the floor.

Was the yellow thing—the pineapple, broken open? And inside was—

"You poisoned my husband, you little hussy, don't even try to deny it!" the Lady Ryder yelled and grabbed Sally's wrists, trying to twist her into some sort of encagement.

"Please, Margaret, really—" Lady Winthrope called out.

"Mama, I doubt—" said the oldest girl, but sounding defeated already. The youngest, suddenly distracted from her thumb, crouched down to pop a piece of half-squished marzipan in her mouth. Her middle sister only just swatted it away in time. Then she picked up a different piece, one that didn't have bits of dirt mashed into it, and gave it to the child instead.

"Mrs. Wade!" Sally yelled. It was the first time Alice had ever heard Sally sound frightened, even when she'd been kicked by the master's horse or when the hem of her skirt caught fire.

"Are we even sure he's—" interrupted Mrs. Lowry.

"ADMIT IT!" Lady Ryder spat.

Alice's head spun. She focused on the battered yellow fruit, now oozing onto the floor in front of her. It was splattered in red, as if someone had coughed blood onto it. And—something else—

"Can someone please explain to me," Alice declared, calmly but loud as a bellow, louder than a screaming kettle, louder still than a chicken with its neck stretched taut on a stump. "Why there is a man's ear inside this pineapple?"

"But he was poisoned," repeated Lady Ryder for the third time. "I saw her slip something into his drink. It must have been arsenic. It must have!"

Alice had gotten her to agree to let go of Sally's wrists, on the condition that Alice would keep a firm grip on the girl at all times, which Sally immediately agreed to. Alice herded them all back upstairs so they could look at this mess properly, carrying the pineapple—and the sliced off ear—with her.

And there the Lord Ryder was, slumped backwards in his chair, arms flung wide in the narrow, red wallpapered room. Drying blood mottled his throat and white froth flecked the corners of his mouth. He still sat in the place of honour, the head of the table, while the rest of the cherry-wood chairs were hastily pushed away and two of the candelabras knocked over. The plates and wineglasses had been cleared away, leaving only the side plates, the port glasses, greasy linen napkins and some bowls of lavender water for their fingers, as well as some candied licorice as a sample before the dessert. The faint smell of urine reached Alice's nose, and she realized he must have lost his bowels. Notably, he still had both his ears.

The nine women fanned out around the table, staring at him, silent. No one cried, not even his daughters.

"Sally, tell us," Alice said quickly. "What did Lady Ryder see when you served him his drink?"

"I—I—" she gazed wildly around. "Alright, I—snuck in some laudanum, but he asked me to! Before the proper dinner started, he took me aside and gave me this dropper—" she held up a small glass bauble. "And told me to lace his drink with it all night, on the sly like, so that the missus wouldn't see it. He said there was no other way he was making it through this night without getting hen-pecked to death otherwise."

Lady Ryder gasped. "He would never say that!" she insisted, but Alice saw the look the two oldest daughters gave each other. As if they were bone-tired of the family lies, and more. "He was thrilled to come speak to our society about the advancement of knitting machines, and how this promised more work for the female poor." She sniffed hard, as if to underscore her point.

"Mama, just—stop it," the middle sister said suddenly. "You would think you could at least tell the truth on his deathbed, if nothing else. You blackmailed him into coming, and you know it." Then she stopped suddenly, as if aware she'd said too much.

"Blackmailed him about what?" demanded Mrs. Lowry.

"The girl has already admitted to drugging his drink!" Lady Ryder said wildly. "Why are we to believe her when she says what's in the tincture?"

Sally trembled in Alice's grasp, knees knocking audibly. "I swear it's not poison, I swear, miss!" Alice made some soothing noises and gently took the small glass bottle from her, but then hesitated. She could identify the smell of almost anything in the kitchen, plant or beast, but laudanum …

"I can do it," Lady Winthrope cut in, sounding almost surprised at herself. She took a tiny smidgen of it and smelled it carefully, then rubbed the smallest amount on the inside of her bottom lip. "Yes, definitely laudanum," she declared, then looked back at the corpse.

"For God's sakes, maybe it was apoplexy," said Mrs. Lowry. "We don't even know if there's been a murder."

But Lady Winthrope leaned over and smelled the dead man's mouth, opened one eye briefly, then shook her head. "Not according to Mrs. Beeton's—"

"*Book of Household Management—*" intoned Mrs. Lowry, Mrs. Beckett and the Lady Ryder at the same time. Apparently Sally hadn't been the only one to notice the mistress's obsession.

"Yes, well," Lady Winthrope continued, seemingly more taken aback by this lack of grace on her friends' part than by the murder in her dining room. "She says that apoplexy would leave one side of the face slacker than the other, with dilated pupils. He has neither. The frothing at the mouth certainly suggests poison, rather than overdose. And ... I could smell the laudanum on his breath." She snuck a quick glance at Lady Ryder as if in apology.

"See! See!" Sally shouted, before Alice could hush her. "And the ear! Where did the ear come from?"

All nine women looked at each other. They all had their ears.

Alice examined the appendage more closely. It was a clean slice—not a hack job or something done in the heat of a fight, but more like the work of a butcher. Or a cook.

Something about it, though, looked ... familiar. She thought it was a man's ear, complete with sprouting hairs and a few freckles. Teeny tiny ones, on the inside lobe, like a sprinkle of cinnamon.

"So ... we can arrive at one conclusion," said Mrs. Beckett with relish. Her attitude had shifted entirely from one of disapproval to one of avid interest. "Someone murdered the Home Secretary of Britain, the Lord Ryder, right in front of us, after sneaking a human ear into the object his wife brought with her as a gift to this household. And that the murderer—or *murderess*, I should say—had to be one of us, here tonight."

Nausea threatened to swallow Alice whole. The others glanced at each other, eyes suddenly hard and suspicious, shifting their weight from foot to foot.

"Isn't this straight out of a penny dreadful!" Mrs. Beckett said delightedly, and rubbed her hands together. "Now, if we can only discover whose ear that is, we shall have a real clue."

"I know whose it is," Alice said in a jagged voice. "This ear belongs—or should I say, belonged—to my son."

Well, that caused an uproar. In a rare moment of household solidarity, Lady Winthrope dragged Alice and Sally to the brandy room, speaking loudly about this being confirmation of a murderer in their midst and each must stick to their own. The other women, muttering, broke into camps: Lady Ryder and her daughters to the parlour, while Mrs. Beckett and Mrs. Lowry stayed with the body.

"What do you mean, your son's?" Sally gasped once they were ensconced in the small room, supposedly kept masculine with navy silk wallpaper and frowning ancestral portraits. Alice perched on the narrow couch, faded and threadbare in spots, and covered her face with her hands.

"Indeed!" said Lady Winthrope. "This is simply scandalous."

Suddenly Alice bit back a laugh. Scandalous! Scandalous!

"I thought your son was taken aboard a ship, pressed into service by the Navy," Sally said gently, but from a distance. As if talking to someone she didn't really know. "Weren't you going to meet him tonight?"

"Yes, I was," admitted Alice, "but he wasn't pressed onto a ship. He'd gotten himself mixed up with bad business, and I told him to keep it far from me. I told him ..." She struggled for words.

He'd still been young, back then, with fast fingers and a knack for the loom. It was his father's trade, and his father's father's before that. What he'd wanted most was to make enough money so that his widowed mother could rest her aching back, leave service once and for all. But then the machines came, and suddenly these devil-crafted machines of metal and steel could do his work five times over in one day. And he was left begging for pennies on the wharf, searching day after day for a few hours' decent work.

Most of all, Alice remembered the way he used to hold a bolt of cloth he'd woven with his own two hands. Back straight, eyes full of the pride that can only be earned, not bought—like Sally's, setting the top piece on that pyramid of marzipan. Even like Lady Winthrope's, finally putting her knowledge as mistress to good use. It was the pride she herself felt when she dressed the venison with a glaze of her own making, of honey and sage and crushed walnuts, and the juices ran clear from the meat.

"I told him not to come near me until he came to his senses," Alice said wearily. "And so I didn't see him for two years. And in that time ..."

The stories in the papers. The broken glass, the figures that staggered from factories engulfed in flames.

Sally pursed her lips thoughtfully, though Lady Winthrope looked completely befuddled. "Luddite?" the girl guessed quietly, and Alice nodded.

"He wanted to meet tonight," Alice said quietly. "I thought this meant he'd come to his senses. But it seems he only wanted to get me out of the house."

"A violent rebel," Lady Winthrope spat out, and stood up abruptly. "You dare bring the scheming taint of those *machine-breakers* into my home?"

That made Alice stand and look her mistress dead in the eye. "My lady, I think you know well enough about *scheming* not to throw the first stone," she hissed, while Sally drew back, both fascinated and appalled.

From behind the closed door of the parlour room, Alice heard a plaintive wail of "Mama!" and a heavy thunk, as if furniture was being knocked over. She instinctively turned to look, though of course the door was closed, until the sound of something wet and sucking drew her back around. But as she did so, she felt as though she were moving through sludge, through porridge, drowning in thick slop that was doing its best to keep her from seeing what there was to see.

Sally's brown eyes. Pleading. Sally, whose eyes had only ever danced with relentless mirth until today, when they'd been beaten down so many times in a row. Sally, in whose open mouth hung a red bubble of blood like a ripe apple roasting in the mouth of a boar.

The Lady Winthrope shuddered as she pulled the knife out of Sally's back, where it had no doubt pierced a kidney, the stomach, a lung.

"That was horrible," she said, shuddering. "I cannot believe you forced me to do that."

"Me?" Alice whispered.

"You've always been so good at keeping your mouth shut," the Lady Winthrope said, pouting. "Why did you have to change that now?"

Too late, Alice realized dimly that Lady Winthrope had moved to stand between Alice and the door. Behind her lay the parlour couch and the bay windows, although they were firmly shut against the late winter air. And Sally, in a pool of blood, still on the floor beside her.

She backed away regardless, anything to put distance between her and the knife.

"How did you know?" Lady Winthrope asked, casually, as if asking what Alice suggested for Sunday dinner. "I don't know why, but somehow the cooks always seem to figure it out, in the end."

"The ledgers," Alice rasped. The only thing she could think of to delay the inevitable was to tell the truth. "The cooks take care of ordering the salt, the sugar, the meat every week. We have to keep clean ledgers, or we'll be accused of theft. Sooner or later, any cook worth her salt would be bound to notice the inconsistencies."

The penciled-over entries, changed ever so slightly after the fact. The overly-complicated household accounting. How money flowing in never seemed to square with money flowing out. The mounting debts became clear soon enough.

"How long have you been running from debtor's prison?" Alice asked.

"Ten years now and counting," Lady Winthrope said. "Lord Winthrope does love his gambling. Every time the debts became too obvious, we moved cities and started over. It was easier in continental Europe. But we missed home, after so long away."

Her eyes gleamed suddenly. "But now! These weaving machines are finally giving us our chance at paying our way out of debt and back into decent society! Lord Winthrope was the first to see the potential in the new textile factories, it's true. But I was the one who saw that if we forced the weavers to rent the frames they work on from us, we barely need to pay them any wage at all."

"Keeping workers like my Ned in poverty all his days," Alice said. "Did you kill him too? After you cut off his ear?"

Lady Winthrope's eyes narrowed, quick and harsh, and she tightened her grip on the knife. "I would never do something so base," she said daintily. "You're the one who poisoned that man out there, the one man who was ready to defend our rights in Parliament and punish machine-breakers like your son as they deserve!"

There was something in the way she held the knife. A warble to it. And Alice saw she wasn't the one who cut off Ned's ear so cleanly. She'd stabbed Sally once Alice had been stupid enough to allude to their secret in front of her. So, so stupid of her. She may never forgive herself for that. But Lady Winthrope still held the knife inexpertly in hand.

Well, Alice thought. Do I know how to use a knife, or don't I? And she wasn't afraid anymore.

She rushed forward, not worried about grace or style, simply overpowering her. Lady Winthrope yelped and jumped back, slashing the knife, but now Alice ducked under it and twisted the Lady's wrist with one iron-strong hand, and caught the falling knife with the other. She quickly twisted the other woman around, and this time she pointed the knife at her mistress.

"Help, help!" Lady Winthrope shouted at the top of her lungs, while Alice blinked. "She's got a knife, please, oh, help!"

The parlour door slammed open, and Mrs. Lowry pushed inside, holding a small ladies' pistol steadily in front of her. "Let her go!" she demanded while Alice gaped. Lady Winthrope wriggled away, falling first to her knees, while Alice dropped the knife. That's when Mrs. Lowry saw Sally's body, twisted on the floorboards, and gasped.

Lady Winthrope flew up and to her friend. "Oh, thank heavens!" she shouted. "This woman did it—she confessed—her son is one of those frame-breakers! Then she stabbed her accomplice right in front of me to keep her quiet. Oh, Mrs. Lowry, it was awful!"

"Stay back!" Mrs. Lowry said through clenched teeth, pointing the pistol straight at Alice.

Alice couldn't think of a single thing to say that would convince this rich, high-born woman that it was Lady Winthrope, not the cook, who did it. "I loved Sally," was all Alice managed to whisper before her vision blurred in front of her and she could no longer breathe.

"... constables are on their way," she dimly heard another voice say. Perhaps one of the Ryder girls.

"Just terrible," Lady Winthrope was repeating, over and over. "In my house! Under my roof!" Mrs. Beckett's voice floated through then, reassuring Lady Winthrope and telling her of a friend she knew, who made a ha' penny per person to come view the spot in her back alley where a man was strangled to death late one night. "Really?" Alice could hear Lady Winthrope saying, further away now. "That much?"

Mrs. Lowry slowly eased further into the room. "I supposed you killed him because of the law," she said to Alice.

If Alice strained, she thought she could make out the clopping hooves of the constable's carriage. "What law?" she asked, so tired.

"The Frame-Breaking Act," Mrs. Lowry repeated. "The one the Home Secretary, Lord Ryder, sponsored. It decrees that the destruction of mechanized looms, stocking frames, or anything of the sort is to be punishable by death. I suppose you were worried about your son, and hoped to stop it?"

Alice had to think through her words, one by one. She was a cook for a household desperate to appear wealthier than it really was. She had no time to read the papers or follow acts of Parliament. Though her chest did constrict at the thought. Punishable by death? A capital offense?

"Not ... her ..."

The two women looked down in concert, and Alice dropped to her knees. Sally! She was alive!

"Not ... Missus ... Wade ..." Sally croaked out, eyes still shut. "Lady ... Winthrope ... stabbed ..." Then she fell silent.

"Sally," Alice said and pressed her hands belatedly to the wounds in her back.

Just then a loud crash sounded from the other room, and everything next happened very quickly.

Sally groaned, Mrs. Lowry yelped, and Alice jumped to her feet. "Put pressure on the wound!" She said to Mrs. Lowry, and held out her hand for the pistol. Wide-eyed, the other woman nodded, and Alice palmed it while Mrs. Lowry quickly pulled a throw down from the sofa nearest her and turned her attention to Sally.

Alice went back into the dining room. The thin little girl was screaming now, her mouth smeared with marzipan, and the oldest daughter was wrestling with Lady Winthrope over what looked like a piece of paper in a mess of heavy silk and green cotton and blue wool. Lady Ryder seemed to have fainted. She was tucked into a chair facing the corner, like a classroom dunce. The middle sister's doing, no doubt. She held her younger sister close, trying to soothe her, while shouting instructions to the older one: "To the left! There! No, your knee, watch your knee—"

Then Alice saw the gleam of the knife, at the same time as the middle sister inhaled sharply. It was the same knife—Lady Winthrope must have palmed it after Alice dropped it and before leaving the brandy room.

"Stop!" Alice shouted, once, and yanked Lady Winthrope back. Lady Winthrope did not stop. She pivoted and leapt towards Alice, knife out, slashing, catching Alice's right wrist. But not before Alice pulled the trigger.

The shot was louder than anything she'd ever heard before. It rang in her ears for what felt like hours, but which was probably only moments. Smoke stung her eyes. When she opened them, Lady Winthrope lay thrown back, eyelids fluttering, her hand to a blossoming red patch at her hip.

"He'll hang," she whispered. "They all ... will hang."

Panting, Alice pushed through the hazy veil threatening to envelop her to pick up the piece of paper laying on the ground. Beside it, bizarrely, was Ned's ear. She clutched both. The piece of paper was gluey with almond paste, drips of fat, and other sundry leavings on the kitchen floor downstairs where it must have fallen. On it was written: "Listen now, or else," in a familiar scrawl. Then there was a poem, slant-rhymed, that ended "We will rise up, and will we not be refused."

"He is a fool," Alice said with much love, and a pained heart.

"He is, isn't he?" said Lord Ryder's oldest daughter with soft eyes.

"She found that note when she snuck back downstairs for more marzipan," Alice's hitherto-unknown daughter-in-law explained quietly, out of earshot from the others. "When she showed me, I realized what he'd done. He wouldn't tell me what he had planned. The idiot. If he'd told me, I could have saved him a perfectly good ear." She shook her head ruefully, but smiled, as if this were all an eye-rolling but terribly funny jest. She hid the note carefully in hand.

The constables were taking note of the bodies inside, tracking mud and blood all over the Turkish carpet. To Alice's surprise, Mrs. Lowry told the constables exactly what Sally had told her—that it was Lady Winthrope who attacked her. And Mrs. Beckett testified that Lady Winthrope had gone after Alice with a knife. After all, she had the slashed wrists to prove it. Alice was beyond grateful that they thought Sally would live—and even grateful that Lady Winthrope would, hopefully, as well. Lord

Ryder, however, stayed dead.

"I didn't kill Lord Ryder," Alice said softly. "And neither did Lady Winthrope, since she stood to gain from his bill in Parliament." She hesitated, then forged on. "I am to take it that you killed him, then? At Ned's command?"

Ned's wife—"Lady Ludd," she'd told Alice to call her—scoffed, but her eyes were ice cold. Her younger sisters drew up close to her, and Alice felt the temperature of the room drop. "No," she said firmly. "That was our own plan." She and the middle sister's eyes met, then glanced down at the feathery hair of the youngest. She watched them all with owl eyes, prepared to flinch at any moment. "For personal reasons." She stopped, then shrugged. "Mother was actually right, for once," she said. "There was arsenic mixed in with the laudanum, although of course that serving girl didn't know it. We didn't know exactly when it would build up enough to take effect. The more he dosed himself, the more he hastened his own death."

Alice drew back, measuring the distance between them. Lady Ludd cocked her head at her.

"Ned would still like to see you," she said. "He still loves you."

"And I him," Alice said. "But I can't ... this isn't right. Tools change, times change. Many people have already gotten hurt. Like *that serving girl*, as you called her. Sally. She almost died, and she had nothing to do with any of this! Please," she begged. "This must stop."

"The movement is bigger than the two of us," Lady Ludd said. "People are starving. Starving people do desperate things."

"Then let me feed a few of them, and come up with a better plan," Alice insisted.

The younger woman was quiet a long moment. She cracked her fingers, looked down at roughened palms. The middle sister looked carefully away, trying to give them some privacy.

The constables were headed their way. Behind them, Lady Ryder seemed to finally be waking up from her faint. Alice shrank instinctively away from them all. This wasn't going to be easy, even with the word of two ladies of good standing behind her.

"Let's talk about this more, over dinner soon," Alice's daughter-in-law said in a rush. Alice nodded. "There are at least small ways to make the hard things easier," she said, and turned to face the constable.

CONCRETE

George Guthridge

I started drinking after my wife left me. Okay, I started drinking *harder* after she left me.

The beginning of the end was at the Springfields' patio party. Gregory Springfield was 48, six years older than me. His wife, Sandra, was 47, a quarter-century older than Arielle. They lived in the ranch-style next to our Cape Cod. The two houses were typical middle-class homes, separated from the rest of the neighborhood by three vacant lots where henbit and purple deadnettle ran savage until I'd get fed up and mow and play Rambo with my weed sprayer.

Arielle and I had moved in six months earlier. A chance backyard meeting with Gregory led to my ripping up their dry-rotted deck and replacing it with a concrete patio that included intricate patterns I'd set into the wet cement. I owned a small concrete business and gave the Springfields a great price.

There were the four of us at the party. Gregory rocked some T-bones on the barbeque, I tossed the salad and brought out the condiments, and Sandra and Arielle finished with the squash and roasted asparagus. Gregory and Sandra were knocking back scotch and sodas, I had too many Coors, and Arielle had polished off a large can of Foster's and was on another. She often said Foster's made her horny. She was beautiful and had a hard body toned by daily Pilates. Startlingly inventive in bed. I kept our fridge stocked with Foster's.

Gregory proposed a toast. "To the patio!"

"The patio!" we all chimed in.

Sandra lifted her glass. "They say the world's running out of water. May the four of us *never* go thirsty!"

We agreed. Wholeheartedly.

She gave Gregory a coquettish smile. I sensed there was more to the toast than alcohol—something I wouldn't understand for another two months.

The small talk swung round to hobbies. Arielle mentioned her Minion collectibles, and said, "And John has his Coors." Everyone laughed—me, to be polite, my teeth gritted.

"Sandra has a collection of first edition Agatha Christies," Gregory said. "She keeps them in the window of her bookstore, along with her signed editions of Ann Rule." When the name didn't register with Arielle or me, he added, "The true-crime writer."

Which turned the discussion to crimes here in Gilman. The boy found strangled in a field; his mother's live-in boyfriend confessed. The Tibbetts girl's disappearance. She lived six blocks away and vanished on her way home from high-school basketball practice. Her mother insisted she hadn't run away, but Gregory was president of the Gilman Bank and Trust and privy to city and police administration conversations. "She had a history of taking off," he said. "As usual, the newspapers went for sensationalism instead of facts."

"This is supposed to be a *summer* party," Sandra said. "Let's be upbeat!" She retrieved a gift from a shelf beneath the serving table, and, coming up behind Gregory, covered his eyes with one hand and presented the package with the other. It was wrapped with blue and white paper and had a pink bow. "Surprise! Happy patio!"

Gregory opened the package. It was a tiny yellow cement truck. A former Ohio State linebacker, Gregory was large and muscular. The toy looked minuscule in his hand. He laughed and kissed his wife.

"It was Arielle's idea," Sandra pointed out.

He thanked Arielle.

"Don't I get a kiss?" she asked.

He leaned forward awkwardly, a hand on her thigh to balance himself, and gave her a peck on the cheek. She reciprocated with one on the lips.

Just the Foster's, I tried to assure myself. But I wasn't happy.

"It'll look great on your fireplace mantle," I said.

Sandra glared at the back of Arielle's head. But then Sandra's mien changed, as if she consciously broke from jealousy's shell. "Mantle schmantel!" she said to Gregory. "They're our neighbors, and they don't know your dirty little secret?"

I looked from him to Arielle to Sandra, who rose and tugged Gregory by the arm. "Come on, show them."

After hemming and hawing, Gregory led us into the house and down the basement steps. Arielle stumbled and half-collapsed into his arms. "My," she pinched a biceps. "And you run a bank all day."

Worry seethed along the edge of my mind, and cold fire flared in Sandra's eyes, but when Gregory looked her way, a switch flipped. Gooey-eyed, she eased Arielle aside and wrapped an arm around his neck, her lips nuzzling him as we descended the rest of the stairs.

Across the basement was a padlocked door. Gregory opened it. Inside was a room with an HO-scale train set. "It's Gilman," Sandra said. "The way it used to be."

"When we were in high school," Gregory said. "Me here, she in Cleveland."

Sandra chuckled and snuggled against him. "Back when you wanted into my pants but were too inexperienced with zippers."

I admired the railroad. "*This* is your dirty little secret?"

"I wouldn't want people knowing how much time I spend down here." He put the concrete truck in the layout's industrial area. "People talk. Like I'd be taking time away from watching over their money."

"You can watch my money," Arielle said. "If we had any."

I was disturbed she'd mention something like that. Covid had so hurt our business that we were down to one employee—an ex-Marine who went by "Gunny." There were little projects, but several big ones had shut down due to lack of workers. Whenever our income plummeted, Arielle had pointed out, my drinking rose. "Like some sicko inverse relationship," she'd once spat at me.

Gregory showed us the cabinets around the wall, all filled with locomotives, cars, and cabooses. His eyes lit up when he talked about them. Some vintage models, especially the Alco engines, cost him hundreds of dollars, he explained. Others, like his rare George Brown Company flat car, he'd gotten at a garage sale for fifty cents.

"Time, Gregory." Sandra tapped her wristwatch. To us: "He'll talk forever about these toys if I don't shut him up."

Gregory went thin-lipped, like a little kid—a *big* little kid—scolded by his mother. He set the oil car he was holding back in its place.

We left the room. The concrete was discolored near the washer and dryer. Someone had done a half-ass job. "Looks like you replaced some drains," I said.

"Problem with an older home," Gregory said. "Must have been forty years of sludge in there. Sandra and I did the work ourselves. I'm not the best handyman."

"I laid the concrete," Sandra said. "Didn't get the mix perfect." She laughed lightly. "Daddy hasn't been here lately. He'd be displeased. I worked for him through high school and during summers when I was in college."

I didn't understand the reference.

"Klabronsky Brothers," Gregory said. "Over in Cleveland."

"Big outfit." I was careful not to add anything. The Klabronskys were known for more the pouring concrete. Word was they'd put more than one person in concrete shoes into Lake Erie.

"Can't go wrong marrying into concrete," Sandra said, and shot Arielle a look.

I saw the real reason for the toy concrete truck.

"I could give the basement a skim coat," I said. "He'll never know." It would be a chance to earn more cash under the table. "I'll throw in the labor on a nice paint job at no extra cost."

"Might take you up on that." Sandra smiled at me, then eyed the floor and joists in disapproval. "This place is so old. And small. We can afford a bigger home, or have Daddy built us something, but my Gregory is always worried about image." She wrapped an arm around Gregory's arm and gave him an alluring look.

"Small house, low profile," he said. "That's what my father used to say. He was the bank president before me."

I knew that. The whole town knew that.

But the person wanting them to keep a low profile was likely *her* father.

Arielle and I fought that night. I berated her for her drinking and flirting. She held up an open can of Coors, let it drop onto the kitchen floor, walked into the bedroom and slammed the door. The can lay there, beer running out. I didn't mop it up.

Her signals at the party turned to classic excuses. She had to work late at the paper—she was a proofreader—she was going out of town to visit a college girlfriend, her phone died.

One evening I came home and took off my filthy boots and Carhartt coveralls in what families call the mud room. I showered, changed, and padded into the house proper, wanting dinner and the game. It was a Monday, and deep into October. That meant *Monday Night Football* and a few brews while Arielle nestled in my arm, her head on my shoulder.

I called her name. Her car was in the carport, so I knew she was home.

Except she wasn't.

The house felt as though someone had opened a door and swept away our life force. When I entered our bedroom, the drawers of her dresser were opened, with clothes hanging out. Not like her at all. Dresses still on their hangers were thrown across the bed. I jerked open the closet. Her suitcase was there.

Her small one wasn't.

On the doily on the dining room table, tented before the candleholder, was a card. Within the filigrees was my name. I trembled when I opened it.

John,

I won't blame you for being mad. I won't make excuses.

I've found someone else.

--Arielle

PS. I'll call you when I'm ready, and we'll talk.

I burst from the house. I'd wanted to trust her. Except for the after-party fight, I'd never confronted her with my suspicions. I didn't want them to be true. Stupid is what stupid doesn't do, to paraphrase Forrest Gump.

Unless I was dumb and blind, Gregory was behind it. Probably banging her in some hotel right now. I ran next door. Sandra's car was in the driveway, the trunk open. She exited the house, trundling a large suitcase behind her.

"She's gone," I said. "Arielle's gone."

"They're *both* gone." Sandra's face was red with anger. "We were going to Florida. A month in the sun. Well, hell with that! I'm going to my mother's—in Paris."

I helped her put the suitcase in her vehicle. "You knew what was happening?"

"He just told me. Nice timing, huh? Then he left." The bitterness in her eyes were the likes of which I had never seen in anyone before. "Left with *her*. To Florida."

She slid into the car. "I wish you two never moved in." She started the engine and brought down the window. "I wish some old widow lived there. I have since the day we met you two."

"And if they come back?" I clutched at hope. "If they both do?"

"He'll be back, all right. For that damn railroad, if nothing else. And to move his clothes to another house." She glanced behind her to make sure no cars were coming. "When my lawyer gets done with him, he'll want to move to another planet. You don't hurt Sandra Klabronsky and get away with it!"

She roared off. I stood in the street, watching the Pontiac diminish in the distance.

The next day, Gunny came into the office trailer. I was hitting the Coors hard, with Jack Daniels chasers.

"Boss?"

"She's gone," I said to the wall. "That bitch. Arielle's gone."

"Oh." He backed out the door.

By evening I was stuporous. I'd thrown everything off the desk with a sweep of my arm and had given the nearest file cabinet such a kicking it looked bent-over in agony.

If Sandra went to Daddy and had Gregory whacked, so much the better. Just so Arielle didn't get hurt.

Then I had a moment of clarity, like a lull amid a hurricane. I grabbed my keys and coat, drove the concrete mixer over to the concrete plant and had them load me to the max.

I took the mixer home the long way. Didn't want to risk a DUI. It was dark by the time I pulled up at our house. Someone driving by wouldn't notice anything out of the ordinary. I often parked my rig there. I checked out the area to make sure no one was around, and with lights out backed into the Springfields' driveway and then around back until I reached the basement's last window. Like the other basement windows, it was about two by three feet, typical for a home built back in the '50s. Two panes. I smashed open the far one with a crescent wrench. Glass shattered into the basement. I cleared off the ragged glass. Arielle had slit my throat. No sense slicing a hand to add to the pain.

I took the chutes off the truck, hooked them together, stuck the last two through the window, and reversed the barrel rotation. The room was about eight by ten. If I poured in four feet of concrete, that would be 11.85 cubic yards—almost precisely my rig's capacity.

Concrete spewed onto Gregory's miniature town. Then I turned the chute toward the cabinets. Cars fell into the mix like fat, dead dreams, not a one of them undamaged.

"You bastard," I muttered of him.

I used the rig's rake to sluice the concrete forward, replaced the chutes on their rack, and headed back to the office. I cleaned out the barrel, hosed everything down and drove my pickup home. I was as satisfied as when Philly beat the Patriots in the Superbowl.

But I didn't believe it.

Two weeks passed. No sign of the Springfields, no word from Arielle. Empty beer cans littered the living room, the dining table, the kitchen counters. Somehow, thanks to Gunny's efforts, I landed a contract for three strip malls going in up in Toledo. I was so elated I wanted to call Arielle with the news. Except I couldn't.

Without realizing it until I was halfway there, I drove to the bank. I asked if Mr. Springfield was in and, if not, when he could be expected. Juanita Horgalaz said he wouldn't be back for at least two weeks.

"Any way I can reach him? It's important."

"I'm sorry. We can't give out that information."

"I'm his next-door neighbor."

She blanched. "Oh! Is something wrong with the house?"

The image of the concrete in the railroad room flashed through my mind.

"No," I lied. "Personal matter."

"Well, you'll have to wait." She eyed the name above my breast pocket. "... John. The Springfields are in Florida. I can't say where exactly." She added, "Obviously."

Two weeks later, a woman's shrill scream shook me awake.

I pulled on jeans and tennis shoes, grabbed the fireplace poker and a flashlight and ran next door. No lights were on. All the doors were locked. No cars in the driveway; couldn't determine if there was one in the garage. I shone the flashlight into every window I could reach, especially the one where I had broken the window. If it had been Sandra who screamed, why would she care about the destruction of the railroad?

I went back to bed but left the windows open on the Springfield side.

The next day, I came home from work in the afternoon. I don't usually return during the day—like most Gilman tradesmen who don't pack a lunch, I take mine at Lucy's—but some sixth sense told me I should return.

No sooner had I climbed from my pickup than a shriek of a concrete cutter came from the Springfield house. It was a sound every concrete worker knows. Someone was in the railroad room, cutting my pour.

I crept over, thinking maybe I should bring the fireplace poker in case it was Gregory, then thought better of it. I'd had my revenge. Didn't want prison for beating him to death.

So much dust plumed from the basement's broken window that I retrieved my safety goggles from the pickup. I peered in the window, expecting to find Gregory within, cutting his locomotives out of the concrete. But why? Surely they were ruined.

Or maybe, thinking I *should* get the poker if not a howitzer, I'd find some worker being overseen by one of the Klabronskys' goons.

Instead, on hands and knees in that small space, wearing a hooded windbreaker and goggles, head sticking between the first-floor joists, was Sandra Springfield, the room clouded with concrete dust.

Next to her were cold chisels, sledgehammer, crowbar, a 24-inch wrecking bar, and an industrial-grade concrete saw. She'd been cutting a grid every few inches near the far wall and using the other tools to break the grid apart. Looked like she knew what she was doing.

She glanced my way. I ducked aside from the window. The saw started screaming again, and I knew it was safe to watch. She wasn't going to look up while the blade was in motion.

She had torn away the railroad-car cabinet along that end of the wall, exposing the head jamb of a steel door a little under five feet high. I realized what I hadn't seen the other day: Hidden behind the cabinets was a windowless room.

Using the wrecking bar, she pried at the cuts in the concrete and broke away small chunks, exposing more of the door. A room containing—a safe? Most likely. She probably was after money or jewelry that was rightfully hers before Gregory came back and squirreled them away. *We can afford a bigger home*, she'd said.

I hoped she took whatever was in that room. Whatever made Gregory Springfield writhe in pain would bring me happiness.

I watched for an hour. Even brought a couple brews from the pickup. An industrial concrete saw is *heavy*. Sandra stopped numerous times to wipe sweat from above her goggles.

Eventually, she exposed half of the steel door. She went to work on it. She halved it, the concrete saw screaming and sparking, cut off the upper hinge and, after considerable crowbar work, wrenched off the top half of the door and dumped it aside. An oak door was within. It cut easily compared to the metal one. She sliced through the hinge. The door's top half fell inward with a thunk, revealing a room well-lit by overhead lighting.

The room was about eight by eight. It was difficult to see inside. It wasn't the angle. The railroad room was cloudy with dust, and Sandra was in the way. All I could see was the upper half of a large, open safe. It looked filled with money.

She drew back.

I stuck my head all the way through the window to see better.

Gregory was sitting slumped against the safe, money in his lap.

Arielle lay in a fetal ball on a bare mattress.

Neither was moving.

My heart thudded in my throat. "Jesus, Sandra!"

She glared at the window and clambered toward me over the rubble, brandishing the concrete saw and shrieking. "You! You caused this!"

I was too stunned to move. I jerked my head back as the saw roared past me, cutting through the window divider, glass shattering.

I sprinted to my truck, slammed it into reverse, peeled over to the Springfield house and rammed the front end against the window. The window was a couple feet off the ground and matched up perfectly with my grill. In case she wanted to escape, she wasn't going *that* way.

I grabbed my tire iron from behind the seat and ran to the front door as I phoned

911. The front drapes were pulled, but I could see her through the door window, running from room to room, gas can in hand, splashing the walls, the couch, the dining table.

I bashed in the window with the tire iron, wrenched open the door, hoping to get to her before she lit a match.

Everything exploded into flames.

A scream from the kitchen sounded inhuman. Sandra hurtled at me, clothes and hair on fire. I'm not sure if I tried to catch her and help her, or if she knocked me down. The next thing I knew we were rolling on the lawn, me with my jacket off, trying to put out the flames, the stench of burning flesh everywhere, police sirens wailing in the distance.

I passed out.

I awoke in the hospital, arms bandaged, a nurse standing beside me, Gunny in the corner, hard hat in hand, Detective Pickford seated on a chair. Pickford was rotund, with a pencil-thin mustache. I had met him when he investigated a break-in at my shop. A good officer.

"You saved her life," he said.

Pickford and detectives from Toledo, poring through the house after the firemen finished, located a box containing drivers' licenses and jewelry owned by women who had gone missing.

By the time I left the hospital, Sandra confessed. Gregory had kidnapped women and raped them in the hidden room. He and Sandra then vacationed for a month and let the women die of thirst. Returning, the Springfields would haul women they considered lower class out into the woods and bury them. They buried women they considered special, Janica Tibbetts among them, in the basement's laundry area.

"We wanted those women's spirits to live with us," Sandra Springfield admitted.

Pickford visited me at the office. "The box included memory chips showing the women's agonies. Sandra apparently got her jollies watching women die after Gregory touched them."

"If a recording of Arielle is in there, I don't want to see it," I said.

Pickford nodded. "Springfield covered the hidden camera on the second day. From what we've pieced together from the footage and from Sandra's confession, he never intended to kill Arielle. Looks like he was chucking it all for her. His position at the bank, his life with Sandra, maybe even his taste for rape and murder. I doubt Arielle knew anything about his other life. They went down there to empty the safe. Several million in cash. Looks like it was from laundering money through the bank.

Klabronsky money, most likely.

"Sandra was wrapping up things at her bookstore," he added. "She came home for paperwork. Apparently, Gregory and Arielle didn't realize she was there. She heard them downstairs and flicked on the camera and audio. Doing that sent her off the rails—to use a bad pun. She always kept a pistol in her purse. She crept downstairs, confronted Gregory and Arielle, took their cell phones, then locked them in and slid back the railroad cabinet. She set the camera system on long-term record and left for Paris."

"But returned to get rid of the bodies," I guessed.

"She was taking them to where she and Springfield buried most of the women. We've found seven bodies there, plus four in the basement.

I buried Arielle and cried over her. I moved in with Gunny, who'd talked me into attending AA. I often visit the grave. The DA dropped the charge against me for malicious mischief. There's a For Sale sign in front of our house. The realtor suggested I cut the weeds in the vacant lots. I told her to hire someone.

BYSTANDER INTERVENTION

Jackie Sherbow

Notice a potential emergency

It had been an awful day already. My partner, after deciding it just wasn't worth it, had dumped me. I'd woken up in the late afternoon, hungover after another night drinking in our small kitchen. I'd smoked inside and drank whiskey in a dusty bottle found behind the spices piled on our counter, left behind after a long-ago holiday party, until my throat hurt and my voice was hoarse.

But I deserve some fun! I'd spent all day looking for jobs and coordinating the food pantry. They didn't see it that way. My gut ached and my skin felt itchy. I wanted to put my hand gently to their cheek. But I just said, "Fine," and carried myself toward the bathroom. I looked at myself in the mirror: My very long, dirty blonde hair trailed well past my shoulders, and it was greasy—but Jo had trimmed it, so it looked okay. The haircut had originally been expensive, but it felt heavy, then. My T-shirt was low-key designer. I pulled at it, so it would look more casual, disheveled. I hitched my jeans up to my waist, cocked my head. I looked very tired, and I liked that. I looked like I'd been trying very hard at something, like I was beautiful, but didn't care about it.

I guess I saw the breakup coming. Anyway, good riddance to Jo. Jo and their dark hair sweeping across their shoulder. Their small noises upon waking, their birthmark, right near their eye.

Fine.

I was on my way to get a hot dog at 7-11, and a cruller—comfort food that I was adamant about gobbling religiously, even though Jo is vegan. Now I could enjoy as many as I want without interruption! So while Jo packed their things back at the studio, I was leaning up against the blank side wall of the Duane Reade, gathering grime, under a small overhang away from the slight drizzle that was picking up—of course it would rain on me today—half-heartedly fending off grease and crumbs, smoking the last of my pack. Soon, I wouldn't be able to bum the $15 from Jo, the $15 she'd have rather saved or spent on nutritional yeast.

I was watching the street lights turn on, the sky darkening, when a man swayed near me. Very close to me.

As a woman in this neighborhood, something like this happens nearly every day. The details about what happened with Drunk Guy are unfortunately extremely boring because of this. I did get spit at, which was a fun variation, and called some choice names.

Some of them lodged in my body. I found it hard to get mad, and I realized I didn't even disagree.

Delegate responsibility to others

He didn't actually touch me, physically. I don't think. I hope not.

Well, after this delightful encounter, after the whole day and night before, the hot dog and cruller were not settling well. So I leaned my head back against the good old Duane Reade, the paper 7-11 bag dangling from my hand, now weak and, I'll admit it, shaking a bit.

I took a breath and was about to click on a YouTube mindfulness training on my phone. Jo loved this kinda stuff and was always suggesting I tried to be more mindful. Always suggesting I breathe, as though I had a choice over breathing or not. But I could change, couldn't I? My phone was taking forever to load. Maybe I'll just go grab a beer, I thought. Hey, I tried.

Anyway, the point is that after all that, after I was spit at and followed, called a bitch and a slut, and I was just trying to be present, some dude had the audacity to come up to me and ask me how I let someone treat me like that. He said he saw the whole thing. Thanks for the help, then, buddy! What he wanted was for me to go find some police. I said, dude, I would never go to the police.

Then I started quoting Angela Davis. Even though I'm white, I feel she speaks specifically to me and my struggles. Jo always said I should stop saying that. Well, screw them and screw this guy! I invited Audacious Dude to the next Democratic Socialists of America reading group. For some reason he seemed bored after that. Well, fine.

Another great day with my neighbors.

Recognize potential risks

This is where things got weird. Even I will admit that. I just couldn't get the echo of, "How are you going to let someone treat you like that?" out of my mind. In fact, I had stood up for myself, done the right stuff, the stuff I've been trained to do, but there was no talking to Drunk Guy. And even if I hadn't—wow, still bullshit.

So I followed him. I followed Dude With Audacity down Roosevelt, under the trains, toward Sunnyside. Past Jo's and my favorite coffee shop. Past the English style garden city we used to sneak through, furtive, alleys between the houses. Past the food pantry where we'd lifted potatoes and the community composting site where we'd chopped up scraps until sweaty.

One of us would have to find a new mutual-aid group.

I was daydreaming about kicking Jo out via a dramatic Slack @channel post when I remembered Dude Who Had the Nerve. He was turning north on 43rd Street, toward the bridges, the industrial streets heading toward Northern Boulevard. He stopped outside a new-ish apartment building. "Gentrifier," I muttered. He looked around, and I ducked behind a small and perfectly manicured hedge.

Assume responsibility and make a plan

I didn't know what I was doing here, just that I couldn't leave. Walking around aimlessly was so much better with Jo. They always had some kind of fun fact about the neighborhood, some wholesome or not-so-wholesome idea about how to convince me to stop in at a palm reader or duck down an alley, grab my face, and kiss me.

The rain had stopped, and it was now just foggy. Orbs developed around the streetlights and I had the urge to wipe my always-dirty glasses.

I figured I should just head back home. I wondered if I should text Jo. Or maybe I should just give them enough time to get out.

Could I—?

No, they'd made it clear that this was it. I was sure they'd already given me a lot of chances. I just hadn't been caring enough to see …

Enough of that. What's he doing? I asked myself about the guy I was following. The guy who had blamed me.

I was tired of my life just happening to me. The rain throwing me off, the fact that I was so tired, people talking to me on the street, getting dumped. Things piling around me as I leaned against the pharmacy and ate junk food.

Did I deserve better than that?

If I did, maybe I'd deserve …

No. I rolled my shoulders back and stretched my head left and right, cracking my neck. I was going to do something this time. This, at least, I could do. As Audacious Guy walked into his apartment, I slipped in behind him.

Take action

The lobby was garish. There was chrome and fake plants, yellow upholstered chairs and an electric fireplace. There was a mail area, where Amazon boxes leaned against each other. Ugh. Some were halfway broken down, and a box cutter sat on top of the mailboxes.

Perfect.

I swung by in a quiet loop and grabbed the box cutter. Then I got into the elevator behind Audacious Guy.

He looked at me, a little strangely. "Um, what floor?"

"Don't you remember me?"

"From earlier? Shit. You look … wet."

I frowned and shook my head, feeling rainwater slip through my collar and down the back of my shirt.

"Why—" I started, then shifted in my squishy shoes. "Why were you giving me a hard time earlier?"

He just stared at me.

"Hey, asshole! Why were you giving me a hard time earlier?"

"Ma'am, I just thought that guy should've had some consequences."

Ma'am!? "Well, I think *you* should have some consequences," I said.

Nice.

And I moved forward in the elevator and slashed at Audacious Guy's beefy neck. Inexpertly, but good enough. He stared at me, shocked.

"How are you just going to let someone do this to you?" I asked. I bet he wished he called the cops on me now.

He fell to his knees, and then all the way to the ground, which was carpeted in a disgusting teal. Then the elevator binged onto the fourth floor.

I thought I better kick him out and then ride back down, but he was too heavy. I ended up just letting the elevator close in on him. Who knew where it would be called, who would find him. Like I cared. His hat, which had fallen off, was stuck in the door, not letting it close. So I grabbed the hat and on a whim stuck it on my head.

I trotted down the stairs, humming Jo's favorite song.

I passed by the mail room and realized I was still holding the box cutter. So I cut down the rest of the empty cardboard boxes. Red drips coated the stupid Amazon smile logo.

Nice. Maybe I could commission a painting of this image.

Follow up and leave safely

On my way home, I passed the community garden, where I tossed the hat into a big bulging bucket of compost and the box cutter, wiped off and rained on, into a toolshed.

By now, the night was getting cooler. I felt crystal. I felt my phone binging, but I didn't check it. My wireless headphones told me they were dead, and I threw them on the ground.

Then I ran back, snagged them, and put them in my pocket. I stared into the garden beyond the fence. It would work out okay, wouldn't it? So far, it always had— for me.

I didn't know what I would do next. But I knew that I was making the world a better place. I knew Jo would take me back. And I knew that I was worthy.

TOUGH NUTS

Melodie Desmond

"I'm not driving back in this rain," Mike said as they got into the unmarked car.

"So what do you want to do?" Ron asked, wiping the water off his fedora.

"I could use some dinner. There's supposed to be a pretty good restaurant across the street."

Mike turned on the car and set the windshield wipers on high.

"A good restaurant here?" Ron said with a sniff. "And since when do you know anything about The Hammer?"

"I don't. I asked one of the doctors. Unlike you, I actually speak to people."

"Highly overrated pastime."

"Looks pretty nice," Mike said, looking across the street from the hospital parking lot.

"If you want to eat with mobsters."

"Why do you have to be like that?"

"Oh, come on! La Paloma. In Hamilton. Need I say more?"

"I'm hoping not." Mike pulled across the street to a parking spot in front. "Are you coming in or are you going to keep six while I go into this den of iniquity?"

"Rule #1: Never leave your partner out to dry." Ron made a dash from the car to the front door of the restaurant.

They were seated immediately, directly beside a man and a woman who did not look like they belonged together. Unless there were very big fees for equally discrete services being exchanged.

"You know you're staring, right?" Mike said.

"Sorry. I'm just tired," Ron said, looking back from the young and remarkably attractive woman.

"Long day with very little return. I get it. If it wasn't so obvious, I'd be staring too. I still don't know why we couldn't have one of their D's take the statement. Our guy's in the ICU. He's not going anywhere."

"Because it's a Toronto case and I'm the OIC and I don't want some townie copper messing it up."

"Ouch. Testy or hangry? Either way, what are you having?" Mike looked at the menu. "I'm going to start with a glass of the house red. Or do you want to split a bottle?"

"You're the one whose driving," Ron said. He looked up just as the server arrived. "I think I'll have the Rigatoni alla Bolognese. And a glass of your house red, please."

"Same," Mike said as he handed his menu to the server, somewhat disappointed that Ron hadn't ordered a bottle.

"Now you're staring," Ron said. Mike was looking at the immaculately dressed older gentleman at the table beside them.

Before Mike could respond, the man slumped face-first into his plate of pasta, knocking his empty wine glass to the floor.

Without thinking, Mike leapt up, pulled the man up with one hand and put his ear to the man's mouth while checking his jugular vein with the other.

"He's got no pulse. Call an ambulance!" Mike directed Ron, who already had his cell phone out.

Mike slid the man down onto the floor and began CPR while the young woman the gentleman had been with stood up, screaming.

"They're on their way," Ron said. "And this is why I didn't want to come to this restaurant."

Three tables away, another two people were quietly talking to themselves.

"Crap, Gina. How do we get out of here?" Nico held up his cloth napkin and peeked around it at the murder scene.

"Damned if I know," grumbled Gina. "Honest to God, Nico. Our family sucks. WHY does this happen every time we go to Uncle Vito's restaurant?"

"Tch tch. You're not being fair." Nico dropped the napkin and stole a full-on glance. "It's only happened once before."

"And that wasn't my fault either!" said Gina. "I do my best to avoid murder scenes. You know that. First rule of the family ..."

" 'Never get caught in a room with a dead body,' " said Nico, nodding his bleached blond head. "I know. But we didn't have a choice this time."

"And now the cops won't let us leave the crime scene," said Gina, putting her head down on the table. "Who are these guys anyway? I've never seen them before."

"Can't be local," said Nico, craning his neck. "I know all the local cops." He shivered from experience. "Not that I've done any B&E's in a donkey's age," he added quickly.

Which made Gina think, how long do donkey's live? Not that it mattered. And where did metrosexual Nico pick up that antiquated expression? That didn't matter either. What mattered was Pete.

"Pete is going to kill me. We just got engaged, after all. And I promised to stay away from all family business. I *promised!* And now this." She groaned theatrically.

"Do you know who it is?" said Nico, craning his neck.

"Not looking. I'm done with looking." She was done with the whole family, truth be told.

"I'm getting up." Nico rose from the chair.

"No! Nico, no—don't get involved!"

But he was already sneaking over. Nico was almost to the handsome cop's shoulder before anybody noticed him. He stood with his hands in the pockets of those slim black jeans, looking down at the body. Nobody said a word at first. And then she heard Nico's intake of breath.

Gina shot up from her chair and dashed over. Both cops stared as she rushed to the scene. She didn't miss the appreciation in the good-looking cop's eyes, but that didn't distract her from the body.

"Crap. Is that who I think it is?" she said. This was not good.

"Big Al," said Nico, shaking his head. "With a face full of pesto. Who woulda guessed it?"

"And just who is Big Al?" said the handsome cop. "And while you're at it, who are you?"

Nico actually blushed. "I'm nobody."

"Oh for goodness sake ..." Gina rolled her eyes. "He's Nico Ricci, my cousin. Owns the Interior Design business next to my jewelry store in Hess Village. I'm Gina Gallo."

"Soon to be Gina Monroe," said Nico.

Gina glared at him.

The bigger cop lurched to his feet. "This a common thing, changing names?"

Nico snorted. In fact, it was. Gina had a drawer full of passports. But this time was actually legit.

"Nope, he's just being a dope," said Gina. "I just got engaged. To Pete Monroe, the sports reporter for The Spectator. You know him?"

The two cops looked blank. "We're from Toronto," said one.

"You'd like him," said Nico. "He's not even family. I mean, he's family in the sense that he's engaged to Gina now, but he's not—"

Gina swatted him on side of the head.

"Ouch!" he squawked.

That got a wry smile from the handsome cop. "I'm Mike. Detective Mike O'Shea," he said. "He's my partner, Detective Ron Roberts."

"This is a pure organized crime hit," Ron said, sotto voce.

Mike cocked his head and looked blankly at his partner.

"The locals are going to take it over once they get here anyway, so I say we write up our notes, hand everything over, and get out of here as quickly as we can."

"You'll have to pardon my partner. He doesn't get out much. So, you know the deceased? And congratulations on your engagement. Your fiancé must be a very good writer to be able to afford a ring like that. Unless he bought it from your shop?"

Mike had no idea how much a ring like that would cost, but picking up on Ron's suspicions of this being a mob hit, thought asking a few questions worth a try.

"Thanks," Gina said. "He is a good writer, but enough for this? No. Not even if he bought it with the family discount. He inherited a lot of money recently."

"I bet he did," Ron muttered, crouching down to take a closer look at the body.

"What's that supposed to mean?" Gina said. Her blood began to warm beyond its usual Italian heat.

"Nothing. My partner didn't mean anything. Where's the young lady he was with?"

"I think she went to freshen up," Nico said. "Is that an Armani suit you're wearing, Detective Mike?"

"Poison," Ron said as he stood up, sniffing something that he'd dabbed off the body. "Your friend has been poisoned. I think we'd better speak to the girl and everyone who works here."

"That's disgusting," Mike said, looking at the pesto sauce on the end of Ron's pen. "I'll go look for the girl. You go talk to the kitchen."

"You won't find her," Gina said before Mike had a chance to move.

"Oh?"

"I should have recognized her earlier. That's Lucy Lanzi. And she isn't anyone's girl. I'm surprised Big Al was with her. Her brother, Tony the Turd, and Big Al don't get along very well. Nothing criminal, just a personality thing, I think. And Lucy usually listens to her brother."

"Imagine what her life would be like if she didn't?" Nico said with a sparkle in his eye.

"She's ... not so lucky in love," Gina offered, noticing Mike's eyebrows furrowing. "Or good with money, if you know what I mean."

Ron shook his head and walked towards the front window.

"Aren't you going to talk to the kitchen staff?" Mike asked.

"Nope. I don't want anything to do with this."

"We were at the table beside a guy that was, according to you, poisoned. I think it's a bit late for that, don't you?"

"We're off duty. Just a couple of guys from Toronto who—"

"Happen to be cops."

"Who happen to be in a restaurant run by the mob—"

"We don't know that."

Gina flinched. Nico cleared his throat. The other patrons in the restaurant had to have heard Ron's comments, but didn't respond.

"Again, I apologize. My partner seems to think that every Italian from The Hammer is part of a crime family."

"And every cop knows them all. Which is probably what's taking them so long to get here. Probably giving Lucky Lucy or whatever her name is time to get away," Ron said with a huff.

"Is it okay to order food?" a woman seated by the front door with her husband asked Ron.

"I'd stay away from the pesto if I were you."

"Uncle Vito runs a clean shop," Gina said nervously.

"Never been any trouble here before?" Mike asked.

As Nico's mouth began to open, Gina shot him a glance that, if it was anything else, would have killed him.

"No trouble, Detective. No trouble at all," Gina quickly said.

"Mike. Just call me Mike. Either of you ever been in trouble with the police before?"

Nico and Gina looked at each other.

"Sorry. I have to ask."

"No you don't," Ron said. "We're just here to contain the scene. Let the locals do their job."

"Yeah. He's right," Mike admitted, flashing a slight smile at Gina. "I got carried away. Besides, you don't look like criminals."

Both Gina and Nico blushed. Ron rolled his eyes.

"Good. They're finally here," Ron said, looking out the window. "Let's grab a table over there, tell them what we know, and get out of here. I don't care how hard it's raining. We're not getting involved."

Gina worked hard not to look like a criminal. She worked even harder not to **be** a criminal, which was a difficult thing to accomplish in her family.

So when the front door of the resto swung open and her nemesis walked in, she let out a theatrical groan.

Two cops walked in, but the man in question was unmistakable ... very tall, and not quite so thin as he had been in Catholic school. He had a face like a ferret, which turned to a predatory leer when he saw Gina standing there.

"Well, well. Gina Gallo. The girl with the longest confession."

"That's getting old, Spence," said Gina, with a wave of her hand. "We aren't in high school anymore."

"And maybe if you'd just dated the guy back then like he wanted, he wouldn't be constantly on our case now ..." Nico confided far too loudly.

Gina swatted him on the arm. Hard.

Mike couldn't suppress a snort. All eyes turned to him.

Gina sighed and stepped in to make introductions. "Mike, Spence. Ron, Spence. And this is Detective Constable Myers." She pointed to the younger fellow who looked like he might possibly be in need of a shave in a year or two. "Mike and Ron are cops from Metro. They just happened to be sitting here eating."

"In this highly respectable place," added Nico quickly.

Someone made a sound like a donkey. Spence frowned as he took the measure of the other two cops.

"From the Force, eh? What're you doing on our turf?"

"Enjoying the scenery," said Nico, quickly. "And the food."

"The scenery? A dead body? And just why are you cavorting with Toronto cops?" Spence turned a bulldog look on Nico.

"Shut up Nico," whispered Gina.

"Excuse me, Sir," said the young cop. "Shouldn't we look at the body?"

Spence turned in a flash and bent down. "Good God, it's Big Al! Who ordered that hit?"

"Not me," said Nico. "I ordered the cannelloni."

Mike repressed another snort.

"Poison," said Ron. "Pretty conclusive."

Spence straightened and sneered at him. "According to who?"

"Whom," corrected Nico, dodging another swat. "Oops."

Ron shrugged. "Do your own forensics. But I'm telling you, it's poison. Check out the signs."

Spence moved in to check out the signs.

"You have to forgive Spence," said Nico, sympathetically. "We don't get a lot of poisonings in this town. Except for lead, of course."

Mike uttered another donkey snort.

"Nico!" Gina pleaded. "Look, Spence. He was sitting with Lucy Lanzi. Does that give you some ideas?"

Spence looked up. "Lanzi? And Big Al? So is Tony the Turd moving in? This a takeover?"

"Nothing to do with us," said Nico, wagging a finger back and forth. "You know we don't do extortion."

"Nicooooo!!!!" Gina hit a hand to her head. "We don't do ANYTHING!"

Nico turned to face her. "I didn't mean us personally, Gina."

The donkey choked again. Spence just growled. "Hey—where's the broad now?"

Nico shrugged. "She disappeared into the kitchen."

Mike turned to Ron. "So much for your theory of them deliberately giving her time to get away."

"Who?" said Spence, growling. "Who 'them'?"

"I'll go look for her," said Constable Myers quickly.

"Smart man," said Ron.

A door hit the wall with a crash. Everyone looked to the kitchen. A stout curly haired woman charging out with a wooden spoon raised high in her hand.

"Who says my pesto is bad?" she yelled.

Gina rushed forward to hold her off. "No one said it was bad, Aunt Vera."

"They said it was poisoned," added Nico helpfully.

"Are you the cook?" Ron asked, looking cautiously at the raised wooden spoon.

"No, I'm the candlestick maker. Who the heck do you think I am?" Aunt Vera snapped. Gina continued the hold on her aunt's wrist.

"I thought you said we weren't going to get involved," Mike said with a slight smile. "Good catch, by the way, Gina."

"Thanks," Gina said, trying not to blush. "You gotta be fast in this family."

Mike smirked.

"I'd be wanting to talk to her if I were you guys," Ron said, looking toward Spence.

"Thanks, Sherlock," Spence said. "I think I can take it from here."

"Doubtful," Ron muttered.

"Say what?" Spence shot back.

"You don't remember me, do you? Or the case we were supposedly working on together?"

"No … you're not *that* guy … ?" Spence said in disbelief.

"I'm not going to have to punch him out, too, am I?" Mike said, remembering a young detective constable that had been on the wrong side of Ron and ended up on the interview room floor a while back.

"If anyone's going to knock anyone out cold, my money's on Aunt Vera," Nico said, seeing his aunt wrangle her spoon-holding wrist from Gina's grasp.

"Anyone think my cooking killed anyone—"

"What's going on here?" Uncle Vito demanded from the kitchen door.

"The gang's all here, eh, Gina?" Spence said with a wry smile.

"Of course we're all here, you nincompoop. We work here," Uncle Vito said, marching towards them, grabbing the spoon from Vera. "No violence in the front of the house, remember?"

"I think I should just go over there and sit down," Nico said, his eyes now fixated on the body on the floor.

"You stay here," Gina said. "I may need reinforcements."

"This guy, he thinks because he's from the Big Smoke that he can come into my restaurant and insult me," Aunt Vera said.

"You insult my wife, you insult me. You insult me, you insult—" Uncle Vito said, narrowing his eyes as he moved closer to Ron. "Big Al! What's he doing on the floor?"

"Not playing dead," Gina said. "He was here with Lucy—"

"Who let *her* in here?" Aunt Vera said.

"I'm thinkin' it was Tony the Turd," Uncle Vito said.

"Poisoned," Ron said. "Unless this Tony fellow works in the kitchen …"

Aunt Vera's eyes turned to fire as she almost sucked all the air out of the restaurant.

"Tell me more," Mike said, pushing Ron away from both Aunt Vera and Uncle Vito. "Officer safety."

"You're not from around here, are you?" Uncle Vito said, pushing Aunt Vera further away from them all. "What's to tell? Big Al was with Lucy Lanzi. Tony the Turd don't like that sort of thing. Now Big Al's dead. Problem solved. You can go back to your big city now."

"Sounds like a great idea. Let's go," Ron said, moving towards the door.

"Not so fast," Spence said. "You're my prime witnesses. Or maybe my prime suspects."

"I may have to punch this guy out after all," Mike said with a nod.

"No violence in the front of the house!" Uncle Vito said. "Gina, go take the order from that table over there. I got a business to run here."

"It's been a long time …"

"I could …" Nico offered.

"No. Not you, Nico. Gina, you do it. Like ridin' a bike. Or," Uncle Vito said, looking down at the body on the floor, "takin' out a—"

"Bag of garbage. Jeez, Uncle Vito. Do you want me to do that too?" Gina said with a nervous laugh, looking at Mike.

"Big Al ain't no garbage. Lucy Lanzi. Now she's another story."

"But she dresses well," Nico offered.

"If you go for that kind of bargain-basement look," Uncle Vito said, his lip curling. "I would have thought someone like you would prefer something … different."

"I hope you're writing all of this down," Ron said, looking disapprovingly at Spence.

"I know how to run my investigations, thank you."

"So it's only mine that you mess up? Good to know."

"You boys gonna argue over spoiled tiramisu or can I run a business here? Gina, take the order. Vera, back in the kitchen."

"You tellin' me to get back in the kitchen?" Aunt Vera yelled, glaring at Uncle Vito.

"We got customers," he yelled back. "You're the cook. How we gonna run a restaurant without a cook? So yeah, I'm tellin' you to get back to work."

Aunt Vera gave Uncle Vito the side eye and then returned to the back.

"Welcome to *Love, Italian Style*," Nico sighed, noticing Mike's discomfort.

"Now, you boys gonna get this outta here, or is it my job?" Uncle Vito said, giving Big Al's body a nudge with his foot. "Either way, don't matter to me. I just gotta get ready for the dinner rush."

"I don't think I feel very well," Nico said.

"Go back to the kitchen with your aunt," Vito said. "Weak stomach, that one."

"I think my partner and I should probably head over to your station to write up our notes and we'll leave them at the front desk for you," Mike suggested.

"I think you and your partner should stay in the restaurant with all of the other witnesses," Spence countered, motioning to a handful of patrons who seemed oblivious to the body on the floor and the current police investigation.

"I think you're in over your head and it's time to call in your homicide boys," Ron said.

"I think—"

"Gentlemen, please," Gina said, pushing her way between them. "This is a family restaurant, not a think tank. If you're going to go on like this, take it out ba—outside."

Spence glared at Ron, who held his gaze. Mike tried hard not to wink at Gina, who ran the fingers of her right hand over the massive rock on her ring finger.

"Gina! You got that order yet? Your aunt is waiting," Vito hollered from the kitchen. "And boys, get Big Al's body outta my restaurant while I give Tony the Turd a call. I'll get him to come out back and you can have a word with him, Spence. Another … incident … solved."

Gina had picked up the order from the table by the window. Just like old times, except for the body on the floor. There was hardly ever a body on the floor, back in her day.

When she turned around to head to the kitchen, Mike fell into step beside her.

"Is this usual?" She put a hand on his arm and pulled him aside for a quiet word.

"What?" He seemed mesmerised by her sparkly V-neck top. Maybe it was the red sequins that held his attention. Maybe it was something else.

"I mean, do you cops usually allow restaurants to continue serving customers in a place where someone has just died of poisoning?"

Mike seemed to snap out of it. "Holy shit, no."

"Didn't think so. But hold that thought. I want you to come with me." Gina continued to hold his arm and pulled him along to the kitchen, ignoring the bickering of Spence and Ron over the body. They cleared the push doors and met a new kind of chaos. Uncle Vito was on the phone yelling in Italian. Aunt Vera was yelling at the poor busboy with just as much vigor.

The blonde companion of Big Al was nowhere in sight, having no doubt vamoosed out the back door. Nico sat on the steps leading down to the back parking lot. His head was in his hands and she could hear him talking to himself and moaning.

"Funny thing about that back door," said Gina, confidentially. For some reason,

Mike brought out the friendly side of her. "It's sort of like a funeral home."

Mike choked. "What. You mean, you hold funerals here?"

"No, no," Gina said quickly. She paused then, to word it right. "Do you know the Dolce Vita Funeral Home in Hamilton?"

He shook his head.

"Has a back door. You can always tell an Italian funeral home. Certain members of the family always enter through the back door, when going to pay their respects. You can drive right around the back, stop under the portico, and not be seen entering or leaving, if you get my drift."

Mike got it. "You're saying, a funeral is a good place for a takeout. There's a parking lot. It's out in the open."

"Exactly. People know who will be there, after all." Gina was impressed by his quick uptake. She wondered if he could put it all together.

"And by 'back door of the restaurant,' you're suggesting someone could enter and leave without anybody in the front of the house knowing."

"Bingo," said Gina, looking him in the eyes. He had nice eyes, warm and intelligent. She felt a shiver, even though it was hot by the ovens.

"I brought you back here because I want to check something." Gina nodded a head toward the warming rack. "I'm not sure how easy it would be to poison one plate, see? It's kind of out in the open, and you can't count on privacy. Someone could see."

Mike was starting to get it. "So you're saying ..."

"Much more likely that someone snuck in much earlier, and put poison in something already prepared."

"Like pesto," Mike said. Gina could see the admiration in his eyes. She smiled at him, then turned to the giant fridge to retrieve the big container she knew would be there.

"Aunt Vera makes pesto fresh every two days or so, as needed." Gina swung back holding the large glass jar that had once contained imported peaches. The fridge door whooshed shut behind her. "If I were Spence, I'd test this container for poison." She held it out to him.

Mike took it, and held her gaze. "So you're thinking this wasn't a targeted hit. Rather, the *place* was targeted rather than the victim."

Her eyes danced.

Nico had materialized by her shoulder. "But that's terrifying!" he said.

"You're saying Big Al was just unlucky?" Mike looked from Nico to Gina. Nico's eyes were wide, and was that eyeliner he was wearing?

Gina tilted her head. "That's for you to work out. Maybe someone knew he had a penchant for pesto." She turned. "Aunt Vera, can you come here for a moment?"

Vera shuffled over, frowning up at Mike. "He's big, isn't he?" she said to Gina.

"Never mind that. We're testing something," said Gina. She took the jar back from Mike and unscrewed the cap. Then she held out the jar to Aunt Vera. "Does this seem right to you?"

"Who did this to my pesto?" Aunt Vera yelled at no one in particular. "It's not even the right texture!"

"See what I mean?" Gina said with a wink.

Uncle Vito hung up the phone. "Lucy. Where is she?"

"How should I know?" Aunt Vera yelled back, more out of instinct than need. "She skedaddled out of here."

"Well, she's got some 'splainin' to do," Uncle Vito yelled back.

"Says who?" Aunt Vera asked.

"Says Tony the Turd."

"Like he'd be talkin' to you."

"And why not? It ain't me he's got a beef with."

"You brought Big Al in," Aunt Vera countered.

"And this pesto sauce wasn't supposed to take him out!"

The noise in the kitchen stopped, just as if someone had turned the volume off.

"They aren't really angry at each other," Gina explained to Mike. "We're Italian. We just talk loud."

Mike ran a hand through his hair. "And the pesto?"

"Don't you say a word!" Aunt Vera warned Uncle Vito. "Not in *my* kitchen."

Uncle Vito looked tentatively at Aunt Vera and then at Gina.

"Outside. And bring your boyfriend with you."

"Did you forget? I'm engaged now," Gina said, following Uncle Vito into the back, Mike in tow.

"Since when has that ever stopped anyone from havin' a ..."

Mike cleared his throat.

"I'm going to have to caution you, Vito ... ?"

"Vito. Just Vito to the likes of you. And no need to caution. This ain't goin' nowhere. Right?"

Gina nodded and then nudged Mike.

"Okay."

"Good. So, Tony knows Lucy is comin' here with Big Al. He knows Big Al loves basil and is likely to order your Aunt Vera's pesto special."

"It really is quite good," said Nico, who had emerged from behind some bushes and was wiping his mouth.

"Can a man speak? Not everyone knows that Big Al is *very* allergic to pine nuts."

"I didn't know," said Gina.

"Me neither," said Nico.

"And did either of you kill Big Al? No. So listen to the story already," Uncle Vito said. "Big Al orders the special—"

"Why would he order the pesto special if he's so deathly allergic to pine nuts?" said Mike.

"Because Aunt Vera don't put no pine nuts in her pesto sauce," said Vito, triumphantly.

"What????" Nico cried.

"That's how they bonded. Vera is 'lergic to pine nuts too, see?"

"Like Big Al ..." Mike said.

"She can't risk handling them. Chop them, get them on her hands. Too risky."

"So you're saying he had some sort of anaphylactic reaction?" Gina asked.

"Exactly. So, like I was sayin', Tony the Turd had a ... friend ... tamper with Aunt Vera's sauce."

"Someone intentionally put ground pine nuts into the pesto to kill Big Al? I'm going to be sick again," Nico said, rushing back into the bushes.

"Good thing that kid's got another line of work," Uncle Vito said. "But no. He coulda killed Vera. Or anyone else who knows the secret."

"And the cleverness is ... nobody else would be likely to get sick if they ordered the pesto, because it's just pine nuts, after all." Gina's eyes went wide. She exchanged a look with Mike.

"Do you have video cameras back here?" Mike asked, looking around.

Vito shrugged. "Is Sophia Loren my Uncle Rocco's second wife's neighbour's first cousin's hairdress—"

"Yes. Right there," Gina said, pointing up at the camera. They all looked up.

"Someone could have snuck in while Vera was otherwise occupied," Mike mused.

"Shopping!" Gina exclaimed. "Aunt Vera often dashes out the back door for fresh produce before the serving staff gets here. There's a market right across the street. Anyone could park out back and watch for her to leave—"

"It would be nothing to break in," Nico offered helpfully.

"This isn't my jurisdiction, so get Spencer or whatever his name is to seize the tape and it looks like you've found your murderer," Mike said.

"I don't want no trouble here," Uncle Vito said. "I'll get that tape out now and he can take it with the body. Let's go inside. It's getting chilly. Nico! Get out of the bushes. It's time to go inside."

Uncle Vito led the procession back into the kitchen, with Gina, Mike, and Nico following behind. He nodded to Aunt Vera.

"Everything is sorted," Uncle Vito said. "Gina's Big City Boy, he fixed it all."

"Next time you're in town, you come see me in the kitchen," Aunt Vera said with a broad smile. "I'll make something special for you, and you and Gina can sit back here and eat."

"He's not my—" Gina through her hands in the air.

"Are you ready to go yet?" Ron asked, coming into the kitchen.

"Almost," Mike said. "Just helping Vito get the tape out—"

"Don't touch that!" Ron said. "You'll erase the whole thing. Unless that was your intention."

"You sayin' I'm somehow … involved?" Vito said, his finger still on the button.

"It wouldn't surprise me."

"First, you come into *my* place of business, accuse *my* wife of poisoning a customer, and now, you're telling me—"

"Why don't we all just watch the video from here?" Nico said.

"Because this ain't no film festival, that's why!" Vito yelled.

"And it's evidence," Ron said.

"Lemme try somethin' else to get it outta the machine. It's finnicky."

"Wait," Gina said. "Nico's right."

"What?" Nico said.

"Just to be safe, why don't we look at it here? I'll get Spence to come have a look at it with us."

Within minutes, Uncle Vito, Gina, Nico, Mike, Ron, and Spence were crowded around the tiny monitor.

"Are we going to wait for Aunt Vera?" Nico asked.

Ron reached over and pressed a few buttons and, before long, the video was playing.

"I guess not," Nico said.

The quality of the picture was much sharper than the equipment suggested it should be. Within seconds, they saw Uncle Vito unlock the back door and walk in, followed by Aunt Vera. There were several minutes of Uncle Vito and Aunt Vera flailing their arms at each other.

"Just a regular day," Uncle Vito said, smiling at his likeness on the monitor.

"If you marry an Italian, you should expect some theatrics," Gina said, squeezing Mike's arm and then seeming to forget to take her hand away.

"Who's that?" Ron said, leaning in as a woman appeared on the screen.

"That dress works very well for her," Nico commented. "Only a certain type—"

"Shhhh!" everyone said.

They watched the woman open the fridge, and pull out a jar. She opened it, dumped something into it that came from her purse, then shook the jar and put it back.

"It's Lucy Lanzi!" Aunt Vera said, having just joined the group. "I told you, Vito, no good would come of having that—"

"What?" Vito yelled. "Like I invited her—"

"Are you sure it's Lanzi?" Ron cut in.

"There's only one woman who could pull off a dress like that," Nico commented. All eyes shifted to him.

"Of course I'm sure. Look at her!" Aunt Vera yelled. "She coulda killed me!"

"Holy crap," said Spence.

"So you're saying Big Al was the target, and Tony the Turd put his sister up to it ..." Ron asked.

"I thought we weren't going to get involved," Mike said with a grin.

"We're not. We're leaving." Ron stepped back and walked towards the front kitchen door, nodding to Spence. "Good luck with your investigation, Detective. Mike?"

"I'm right behind you. I guess we'll pick something up on the way home."

"Wait," Aunt Vera said. "You allergic to pine nuts?"

"No. Why?"

"Gina, make your boyfriend something nice with this sauce."

"You can't do that. It's evidence," Mike said.

"He's not my boyfriend." Gina removed her hand from Mike's arm.

"Gina, you want to keep a man?" Aunt Vera continued.

"Aren't you engaged to Pete Munroe?" Spence looked Gina up and down.

"Right now she is," Aunt Vera said. "Anything can change. But, like I was starting to say: Gina, you want to keep a man, keep him well fed. Make something nice for him to take away.”

Gina hesitated.

“Go, go, go!” Aunt Vera pointed to the kitchen.

Gina looked back at Mike. He took a business card from his pocket and handed it to her, while never taking his gaze off her. "Just in case that engagement of yours doesn't work out."

Gina couldn’t help it: her eyes twinkled as she took the card. "Thanks!" she said, and tucked it into her bra.

ROAD TRIP

Marcelle Dubé

Cass left the Alaska Highway behind at Dawson Creek. Less than nine hours to go before reaching Calgary.

"Hang on, honey," she murmured. "I'm coming."

In the long shadows of the late November mid-afternoon, Highway 97 stretched ahead of her, an endless panorama of dark green spruce trees, gray pavement and white snow. It was hypnotic.

Shaking her head to clear it, she pushed the Abba CD into the player slot and turned the volume up. *Take a Chance on Me* would keep her awake.

She didn't hear her cell phone ding, but the screen lit up, warning her she had a text. She kept the phone in a holder angled over her dashboard so she could see it easily. She had stopped pulling over every time she got an update from Carter. She hadn't seen another car in the last half hour. She did slow down, however, because she had seen moose on the highway. Yesterday, bison had loomed out of gloaming, so close the damned things almost gave her a heart attack.

"THEY STARTED INDUCING HER. DILATED TO 2 CM."

Hell and damnation.

Lauren had warned her they might induce her, since the doctors were worried about her high blood pressure. It was two weeks before her due date.

Cass already had her ticket to fly to Calgary next week. She would have been there in plenty of time for the birth. But with the change in plans, the soonest she would have been able to fly out was on Wednesday, four days from now.

She couldn't risk it. So she had packed, made sandwiches, and begun the long drive south from Whitehorse. The trip would have taken three days if she stopped at night, less than two if she drove straight through. She had driven through the night, and now was set to drive through the night again.

Maybe not the smartest move, but Lauren was scared, even if she wouldn't admit it. So was Carter. He was a good man, that one. Lauren had chosen well.

The figure jumped out of the long shadows at the side of the highway and Cass swerved in a surge of adrenaline. Thank God the road was dry. Hands clamped on the steering wheel, she glanced at her rearview mirror and saw a girl, her pale hair gleaming in the fading light.

Cass took her foot off the gas pedal as she worked out what was happening. The girl was staring after Cass's car, her figure growing smaller as Cass's Outback got farther and farther away.

Before she knew she was going to do it, Cass braked and started backing up on the empty highway. She stopped next to the slight figure and pressed the button that rolled the window down. Cold air invaded the interior, making her shiver.

"Hi," she said, leaning over to look at the girl. And she was a girl, definitely no older than nineteen or twenty. Lauren was only a few years older. "Do you need a ride?"

What are you doing, her more cautious side warned in alarm. Every single hitchhiker story she had ever heard of or read about flitted through her mind as she waited for the girl to respond. She resisted the urge to feel between her seat and the door frame for the two-foot-long maple dowel she kept there. Just in case.

The kid leaned over cautiously and glanced inside the car before nodding.

"Yes, please," she said. Her voice sounded funny, as if her lips were too stiff to talk properly. She fumbled with the door handle for a moment before opening the passenger side door and sliding inside carefully. As if her body hurt.

For the first time, Cass realized that the girl had no hat, no mitts and only a thin jacket that looked like it had a wholly inadequate layer of down in it.

What the hell was she doing out in this weather? She was so clearly not dressed for it. Cass glanced at the temperature gauge on the dashboard. Minus twenty-three Celsius. Without a word, she rolled the window up and turned up the heat. Then she turned on the heating in the passenger seat. She pulled off the pashmina scarf she'd wrapped around her neck and handed it to the girl.

"Put that around your head," she said. "It'll help warm you up." She took off her fur-lined gloves and handed them to the girl. "And put these on." She glanced down at the girl's feet. Boots. Well, at least there was that.

"Thank you," whispered the girl. She was crying.

Cass smothered a sigh. Honestly. It was a wonder young people survived long enough to procreate.

She thanked the manufacturers for the heated steering wheel. Already she missed the scarf. At five feet and ninety-eight pounds, she didn't have much insulation against the cold. The girl sitting next to her didn't look much bigger.

"Did your car break down?" asked Cass as she finally put the Outback in gear and pulled away. The sun was already down past the tops of the trees. Soon it would be that in-between time she hated so much. Between day and night. Between life and death.

"It's in the ditch," said the girl. Her teeth were chattering. Cass glanced at her but it was too dark in the car to see any telltale white splotches on her face. She thought she saw a bruise on her cheek. Probably injured herself when her car hit the ditch.

"How long were you out there?" Cass hadn't seen any cars in the ditch but she could have missed it.

"I don't know," admitted the girl. Already her voice was stronger and her shivering seemed to be slowing down. "It was really nice of you to stop for me."

"Of course," said Cass with a shrug. "Anyone would have done the same."

"Two cars went by me without stopping," said the girl softly.

Cass gave her a sidelong glance.

"You probably scared them," she said tartly, "jumping out of the ditch like you did."

Out of the corner of her eye, she saw the white oval of the girl's face turn toward her.

"That never occurred to me."

Cass grinned. Then she laughed. After a moment, the girl joined in.

"My name is Cass," she said finally.

"Amber," said the girl. She had pushed the scarf off her head and even in the gloom of the car, her hair gleamed like moonlight. "Do you have a cell phone?" she asked timidly.

Cass shook her head.

"I mean, yes, I have a phone but there's no cell service. There's a gas station about ten miles from here," she added. "Hopefully we can get cell service there. You can call for a tow truck. Or your family."

Amber nodded and turned away to stare out the window.

"Where are you headed?" asked Cass before she could stop herself. Geez, she thought, if she wanted you to know, she would have told you.

But she couldn't help it. There were so many stories of women disappearing from highways. Or being found murdered …

"Edmonton," said Amber. "Or Calgary." She was facing front now and something in her voice told Cass to stop prying.

A flicker in her rearview mirror caught her attention and she looked up to see a pair of headlights approaching from behind. Another hour and she'd be in Grande Prairie—it made sense that there would be more traffic. Finally.

As the vehicle got closer, she flipped her rearview mirror to night vision, even though it wasn't fully night yet. The other driver still had his high beams on. Probably forgot he had them on. The driver was clearly in a hurry. As he approached, he pulled into the other lane to pass her. When he came abreast, he slowed until he was paralleling her. She glanced up but couldn't see anything through the pickup's smoked windows. He wouldn't be able to see anything through hers either.

Just as she was starting to get alarmed at his behavior, the white truck pulled away and sped off.

Cass turned her head to say something about some people being in a hurry and found Amber huddled in the well of the passenger seat, tucked as far under the dashboard as she could get.

Cass pulled into the first rest stop she could find and parked facing the highway. She turned her headlights off and waited, her trembling hands clenched on the steering wheel. Gradually, Amber unfolded herself from the floor and crept up onto the passenger seat, hissing softly as if the movements hurt her.

Cass kept her eyes on the black rectangles of two outhouses fifty feet away, letting the girl regain her composure as best she could.

The sound of the car heater was very loud in the silence.

After a while, still watching the unfolding night, Cass spoke.

"When I was twenty, I met a man, a well-known lawyer. He was thirty-five and very handsome. He loved the opera, and fine dining. He could tell you everything about the world's best whiskeys. Everybody liked him. After I married him, he started beating me."

In the darkness, she could sense the girl's gaze resting on her face.

"I didn't have any family to speak of. And he made sure that my few friends stayed away. I had to quit my job after he broke two of my ribs and my co-workers started asking questions." She kept her voice neutral but inside, her stomach tightened at the memories.

"I stayed with him for three years," she continued. "Three years where I kept telling myself he didn't mean it. He couldn't control himself. He loved me. He wouldn't do it if only I was a better wife. Then, one day, I realized that if I didn't leave, I was going to have to kill him."

She turned to face Amber.

"Who is beating you, Amber?"

The girl stayed silent for so long that Cass thought she wouldn't answer.

"My boyfriend," she said finally. "I've known him since high school. He started beating me this year, after he lost his job. And started drinking."

Cass nodded, familiar with the story.

"When did you leave?"

"At lunch time," said Amber. Her voice was shaking. "After he left to go to the bar."

"Did he cause your accident?" Cass asked softly.

In the darkness, she saw the gleam of Amber's hair as she shook her head.

"No. A moose came out of nowhere and I lost control. I was driving too fast," she admitted.

"Does he drive a pickup?" asked Cass.

"Yes," said Amber. "A white Ram."

"Does it have a cap? A canopy?"

Amber shook her head again. "No."

So. The boyfriend could have been driving the truck that had just passed them. That would explain the driver's behavior. He slowed down to see inside her car. To see if his runaway girlfriend was there.

"Was it your boyfriend who passed us?"

"I don't know," admitted Amber. "When I realized someone was passing us ..."

Cass took a deep breath.

"Do you want to call the police?"

"No," said Amber quickly. "No police."

Cass nodded. She couldn't blame her.

"I'm going to Calgary," she said finally. "You're welcome to come with me."

"Thank you," said Amber. The relief in her voice was unmistakeable.

The girl had no purse with her, no suitcase. No cell phone either. Cass was willing to bet that she had no money on her. She was going to need help.

Cass's cell phone dinged at that moment, its screen lighting up the interior in a ghostly light. Cass leaned in to read Carter's text.

STUCK AT 4 CM. STILL DOING GOOD.

"Trouble?" asked Amber softly as the screen winked out.

Cass sighed.

"My daughter's in labor. In Calgary. I'm supposed to be there."

"Then we should go," said Amber firmly.

Cass smiled. "First, we use the outhouse." She'd been needing to pee for the past half hour. If she didn't use the outhouse now, she'd have to squat by the side of the road later.

Amber laughed softly in the darkness.

"If you open the glove compartment," said Cass, "you'll find a flashlight."

Amber found it and they both got out of the Outback. It felt good to stretch her legs, even if it was wicked cold out. Cass reached into the back seat and pulled a diminishing roll of toilet paper out of her small pack.

"You never know," she explained as Amber trained the flashlight on the battered roll.

Both outhouses had toilet paper but as neither woman wanted to use the facilities in the dark, Cass let Amber take the flashlight into one them while she waited outside, bare hands stuffed in her pockets, collar zipped all the way up. She missed her scarf, but that girl needed it more than she did.

Night had fallen and the sky was awash in stars. She was still staring up when Amber came out.

"So beautiful," she murmured, accepting the flashlight and the toilet paper. "I'll be right back," she added, turning toward the outhouse. She had debated leaving the engine running, but really, she didn't know the girl. What if she took off with the Outback?

She closed the outhouse door and took a moment to flash the light around before setting it down next to the toilet seat. She didn't expect to see any critters—not really— but she had learned to be cautious in her fifty-two years.

She was just finishing up when she heard the sound of a vehicle entering the rest stop area. She hurried to pull up her underwear, long johns and wool pants and rearrange her sweaters and coat, then she grabbed the flashlight and came out.

A white pickup was parked behind her Outback, blocking her. A man stood by her car, peering into her windows.

"Can I help you?" she said sharply, letting the frozen wooden door slam shut behind her.

The man straightened and turned to face her. He was a tall one, at least a foot taller than her. Of course, that wasn't saying much. She trained the flashlight beam on his face, all the while forcing herself not to scan her surroundings for signs of Amber. Where was the girl?

"Hi," said the man in a friendly tone. He was young, no more than thirty, and handsome in a generic way. Dark hair. No hat. "Sorry—didn't mean to be nosy. I just wanted to make sure everything was all right."

He stood between her and the driver's side door. Between her and her sturdy dowel, which now seemed much too small. She didn't think he could see into the car, in the dark, without a flashlight.

"Everything's fine, thanks. Just needed to use the facilities."

"In that case," he said with a grin, "I'll use the facilities, too, and be on my way."

He headed for the outhouses, only to stop when Cass spoke up.

"Would you like me to move your truck for you?"

He stopped and turned back. "Sorry," he said. "My mind was elsewhere."

He loped back to his truck and got in. He parked it next to her car. She noticed that he turned the engine off before getting out. She hid a smile.

"You have a nice evening," he said politely.

"You too," she replied. She watched him head for the outhouses and held her breath until he opened the door to the one she hadn't used and went inside.

So—Amber wasn't hiding in the other outhouse. Where was she? She opened her car door and glanced inside, even though she knew the girl wasn't there. The car had been locked. She must have heard the truck coming and hidden herself. The rest area had been carved out of a forest of black spruce and aspen trees. Ten steps beyond the outhouses, and the trees would swallow anyone up.

She could just wait until the guy left and then call out for Amber.

It suddenly occurred to her that she could do some snooping of her own. Closing the door softly, she turned toward the pickup and flashed her light around. She couldn't be sure this was the same pickup that had passed her. It was white, but this was truck country, after all. There would be plenty of white trucks.

On the other hand, if it *was* the guy who had passed them, he would have had to retrace his steps. Why would he do that, unless he suspected that Amber was with her?

The windows, except for the windshield, were smoked, just like the truck that had passed her and sent Amber into panic mode. But if she pressed the flashlight to the passenger window, she could see inside. Nothing but receipts and old food containers on the seat and on the floor. There was a purse on the floor. What was he doing with a purse on the floor of his truck? Had he taken it from Amber's vehicle?

She moved to the back window and flashed the light around. A black and orange case lay on the seat. It had handles and was just the right size to hold a rifle.

She swallowed hard as she moved to the front of the truck. It didn't necessarily mean anything. This was hunting season. Wasn't it? But the purse ...

The light caught on the metal ram's head affixed to the grille and her heart sank.

Wherever you are, Amber, she thought, stay there.

She needed to take a picture of the guy's license plate before he came back. Her phone was still in its holder in the car.

"See something you like?" asked the man from only a few feet away. She jumped and slapped a bare hand on her chest.

Damn, damn, damn.

"You scared me!" She laughed and aimed the flashlight toward the ground. "I've been thinking of buying one of these, but really, it's too big for me."

He laughed easily. "I'll say. A little bitty thing like you? I don't think you'd be able to see over the top of the steering wheel."

Something in his tone froze the fake smile on her face. *A little bitty thing like you.* That's what Ron used to call her.

"Have a safe trip," she told him and got into her car. She tossed the flashlight onto the passenger seat and took the cell phone out of its holder, exquisitely aware that he was still standing outside in the darkness, staring at her. She desperately wanted to lock her doors but refused to give him the satisfaction.

The screen lit up and she stared down at it.

STILL AT 4 CM. THEY'RE MAKING HER WALK AROUND.

She punched in the camera icon and placed the cell phone on the passenger seat, ready to pull it up and take a picture of the license plate as she drove by his truck. As if guessing her intention, he sauntered to the back of the truck and stood in front of the license plate.

She still couldn't be absolutely sure this was Amber's boyfriend, despite what her gut told her. There were tons of Ram trucks around. Even white ones. And just because he was giving her the creeps didn't mean he *was* a creep. And there might be a perfectly good reason he had a purse in his truck.

She glanced at the clock. Just a little past six o'clock. She hoped Lauren wouldn't still be in labor by the time she arrived in Calgary. At the same time, she wished she could fly the rest of the way and be there for her daughter.

It killed her that her only means of communication was texting. If texts could go through, why couldn't calls?

Out of the corner of her eye, she saw the man move toward her and she put her car in reverse, just touching the brakes to activate the door locks. She ignored his dark figure as she rolled slowly through the rest area, ready to unlock the doors should Amber run out of the trees.

But she wouldn't, Cass knew. Fear would keep her in the trees until her abuser had gone. After that, she would try to flag down another driver. Cass shook her head. Good luck with that.

At least she had a scarf and gloves now.

Cass got on the highway and accelerated. She would head for the gas station. There would be people there. She could get help. Call the police? She sighed and gripped the steering wheel harder. Amber didn't want the police and Cass knew why. She just wanted to get away from her boyfriend. Disappear. Make herself invisible to him. Bringing the police in would make her very visible.

And if she was visible, she was vulnerable. Going to the police would make him angry. And there was no guarantee the police would be able to stop him.

Not until he killed her.

A pair of headlights appeared in her rearview mirror and she released a breath she hadn't known she'd been holding. He must have decided that Amber had gotten into some other car.

Or maybe he had decided to follow her.

She pressed down on the accelerator and the car surged forward. She wanted to be far enough ahead of him that he wouldn't see her turn into the gas station. She would hide behind the gas station until he had driven by and then she'd double back to the rest stop and hope Amber was still there. Alive.

If she were truly honest with herself, she wanted to be invisible to Amber's boyfriend too. He reminded her too much of Ron.

Soon she was driving well over the speed limit, in the dark, in moose country. She had stopped believing in God a long time ago, but now she sent a small prayer out into the universe. Just in case.

She kept an eye on the rearview mirror. She could no longer see the headlights. She had to get to the gas station before he caught up enough to see her tail lights. Leaning forward a little, clutching the steering wheel, she applied more gas and prayed she wouldn't hit a patch of black ice.

Her headlights lit up the road ahead and her side of the ditch. There was a good foot of snow in the ditch. At least it would cushion the crash ...

She kept a nervous watch for lights in the dark, but her luck held. After passing two signs that promised gas soon, she saw the sign for the Petro-Can up ahead and slowed down. She was still going too fast when she turned into the gas station, but fortunately there were no cars and she managed to slow down enough to avoid fishtailing. She glanced around, but saw no one. Then she realized that the inside of the service station was dark.

It was closed.

Move it, her little voice told her, and she drove around to the back of the station before the pickup driver could arrive and see her stopped in the middle of the lot like a ninny. It was dark around back but that was what she wanted. Her headlights picked out empty pallets stacked haphazardly against the trees that came up close to the service station. She turned the engine off and got out of the car, remembering just in time to grab her cell phone and the dowel. Then she closed the driver's side door and counted off the seconds until the headlights finally shut off.

The glow from the Petro-Can sign in front was enough to show her outlines of the barrels and equipment stored in the back. She would not be able to drive out. She would have to back out. For the first time, she noticed the pervasive smell of gasoline. She was surprised she could smell anything, her nose was so cold.

Remembering her cell phone, she put it up to her eye level and punched in her code. To her disappointment, there were no bars.

Just then, she heard the whine of a vehicle approaching on the highway. She dropped the phone into her jacket pocket and gripped the dowel at chest level.

The cold attacked her bare hands, ears, cheeks and nose, though her head was still fine. Time had not been particularly kind to her, but it had left her with a full head of thick gray hair. Good insulation. Her bare hands, however, were going to pay with arthritis pain.

The vehicle turned into the service station lot and slowed to a stop. Cass took a deep breath, trying to control her trembling. The air seared her nostrils and hurt going down. Out front, a door opened and closed.

Cass plastered herself against the back of the service station and closed her eyes tightly.

"I know you're here," called a man. It was the man from the pickup. There was a familiar note in his voice, a gloating note. A note of anticipation. He knew he had her trapped. "I'm not going to hurt you. I just want to check your car and then I'll leave."

Check the car. He was looking for Amber. And if he found her? She would be beaten, punched, kicked. Maybe killed. Her body would be discovered in a ditch along the highway, or maybe never found. God knew, it happened all the time.

She was afraid, she realized. As afraid as when she thought Ron was going to kill her. Back then, the fear had paralyzed her. Trapped her.

She didn't say anything. It didn't matter what she said. She knew he would hurt her. Maybe kill her too. Then he'd search the Outback and when he realized Amber really wasn't with her, he'd go back down the highway until he found her.

What made him think Amber might be with her in the first place? The kid could have gotten in with anyone else driving down that highway.

Not if they were men, she realized. He assumed Amber was with her because she was a woman.

She thought briefly about texting her plight to her son-in-law, but there was nothing he could do. She hadn't even gotten the guy's license plate number.

But he didn't know that.

She pulled her phone out. She would let Carter know where she was and give him a description of the truck and the guy. At least the police would have a place to start looking. In her right hand, she held the dowel against the side of her leg, its hard solidity comforting to her.

"I took down your license number," she called out. Her voice cracked a little. "I've texted it to my family. Anything happens to me, they'll come looking for you." There. That would give him pause.

"Is that so?" he said from behind her.

She whirled in alarm, almost falling as she stumbled back. It hadn't occurred to her he might wind his way from the other side through the machinery and detritus.

"Why don't we just see if that's true?" he said with that same gloating tone. He grabbed the phone out of her frozen hand and swiped through it.

Cass took a step back. Maybe she could make it to her car and lock the doors before he could do anything. Let him keep the phone.

"Now, see," he said calmly. "You just lied to me." He dropped the phone to the frozen ground and stepped toward her. "A little bitty thing like you ought to know better than to lie."

He grabbed for her arm but she slipped away from him, terror spiking through her. He was going to kill her! For a second, she was back in her fancy Vancouver condo, the one Ron constantly reminded her he had paid for, and he was hitting her in the ribs until she fell on the coffee table and broke it, which only infuriated him more.

"Where do you think you're going?" yelled the man, all reasonableness gone from his voice. "Tell me where she is!"

He grabbed for her again and this time, his hand wrapped around her upper arm, squeezing so hard that it hurt, even through her layers.

The pain was like a slap in the face. She had promised herself she would never put up with that again. With that, all the fear swept out of her, replaced by a familiar white-hot rage.

The hand holding the dowel rose as if of its own volition. The man was so busy screaming at her, his face close to hers, that he never saw it coming. She struck him as hard as she could on the side of the head.

He immediately let go of her and stumbled back. She couldn't make out the expression on his face but she could imagine it. Surprise. Shock.

The dowel swept up and down again, this time on the other side of his face. He screamed.

The dowel swept up again. And down.

He tried to fend her off but he couldn't seem to see well enough. At last, he fell to his knees. He tried to say something but she was pretty sure one or two blows had broken teeth.

He raised his head to look at her and she realized that she could see him pretty well. Not well enough to see the fear she knew had to be there. But well enough.

Taking careful aim, she slammed the dowel into his throat.

He dropped to the ground, gurgling and gasping, clutching his throat with both hands. His legs scrabbled against the snowy ground, churning it.

She stood very still, watching until he finally stopped moving, and the sounds finally stopped. Then she leaned over and grabbed a handful of snow. Ignoring the burning pain in her hand, she rubbed the snow all over the dowel even though she couldn't tell if there was blood on it.

There had to be.

Then she searched around for her phone and finally found it, buried under a layer of snow. She wiped it off on her pant leg and slipped it in her pocket. The dowel she replaced between the driver's seat and the door frame. Then she climbed in, started the car and reversed out from behind the service station. As she emerged from the side of the building, it occurred to her that there might be cameras. She studied the front of the building and the pumps, but the only camera should could see was an old-fashioned one mounted above the door to the station. It was trained on the pumps.

Should she break it? She almost slumped with exhaustion at the thought. What if the camera recorded to a computer? What if someone was monitoring the computer somewhere else? What if there was another camera inside?

She shook her head. If they caught her, so be it.

She kept to the edge of the lot as she drove to the pickup. It was still running. She left her own car running, ran to the pickup and climbed in, pulling on her sweater sleeve to cover her hand before pulling on the door handle.

He was right. She could barely see over the steering wheel. She didn't want to adjust the seat, not wanting to touch anything she didn't have to. Stretching her leg as far as she could, she gently depressed the gas pedal. The truck lurched forward. She finally managed to squeeze it in behind the service station. The man lay still, the blood on his face black in the headlights.

She turned the engine off, still with her sweater sleeve covering her hands, and scrambled out of the truck. With any luck she'd be in Calgary long before anyone found him and his truck.

Her hands were still cold by the time she reached the rest stop. She stopped in the middle of the small parking lot and slid out of the car. Her headlights lit the outhouses and a wide swath of forest but everything else was dark. And cold.

She grabbed the dowel and headed for the outhouses. She opened the door to the nearest one. Empty.

"Amber?" she called softly, opening the door to the second outhouse. Also empty. She reached inside, lifted the toilet lid and dropped the dowel inside. It made a soft thunk far below.

"Amber?" she called. "Amber? Are you out there?"

She waited in silence, hoping to hear something but only the cold night answered back.

"Amber, it's all right." She raised her voice. "He's gone."

She stepped into the cone of light, in case Amber was too scared to come out. "Come on, honey, it's too cold to stay out here."

A soft rustle focused her attention on the forest to her right and her adrenaline spiked. Was it a wolf? A moose? She'd heard that moose could be dangerous.

"Cass?"

The relief almost robbed Cass's legs of strength.

"Yes. Come out. It's safe."

Amber stumbled out of the woods, a dark shape against the darker trees. Cass crossed the cones of light to help her to the car.

"Let's warm you up," she said firmly. "What a clever girl you are, hiding from him like that."

She kept up the nonsense chatter, maybe as much for her own sake as for the girl's, until she was safely strapped in and Cass had checked her face and hands for signs of frostbite. She looked okay, but it would be safer to get her to a doctor.

At last she strapped in, too, and they headed back to the highway. They drove in silence for a long time before Amber finally spoke. Her words came out slowly, as if she was working to warm up her lips.

"Did you see where he went?" Her voice was low. She was still scared.

Cass debated telling her everything. If she didn't, the girl would be looking over her shoulder for the rest of her life. But if she did tell her, Cass would be the one looking over her shoulder the rest of her life.

No. It was enough that Amber was safe now.

"He passed me and kept driving. He'll get sick of the road after a while and go back home. You're safe."

By then, they were close to the service station.

In the faint light of the dashboard, she saw Amber turn to face her. "They're going to find my car. They'll connect him to me, eventually, and tell him where they found it."

Cass nodded, her eyes on the road, refusing to notice the empty Petro-Can parking lot. Crap. The purse. They would definitely connect him to Amber.

But maybe they would investigate, learn that he'd been abusing her. Maybe they would assume he had run her off the road.

"They may search for you for a while, but when you don't show up, they'll figure you wandered into the woods and died of hypothermia." Or they might assume that he had killed her and hidden her body, after they found her purse in his truck. As for who had killed him … well, let that remain a mystery.

"If they find you," she said calmly, "you can tell them the truth. That you were running away from your abusive boyfriend, lost control of the car because of a moose and ended up in the ditch. You can tell them that a nice lady picked you up and gave you a ride to Calgary."

"And I'm not sure I'll remember her name," said Amber thoughtfully. "And I'm terrible with identifying cars." Her voice sounded stronger.

Cass nodded decisively. Well, whatever happened would happen.

"We've got a lot of road to cover," she said. "Are you still okay with Calgary?"

"Yes," said Amber. "I think it's time for a clean sweep."

Yes, that was how Cass had felt too.

"Cass?"

"Yes?"

"What happened to your husband?"

Cass breathed in and out a few times before answering.

"He died a long time ago."

Into the pregnant silence, a soft ding alerted her to another text from Carter.
5 CM! WE'RE MAKING PROGRESS!
She smiled. She probably wouldn't make it in time.

MY DEAD-END JOB

Mark Thielman

Today, I consider myself the second unluckiest man at Headstone Haven.

Yeah, I know that's a total rip-off from Lou Gehrig. I paraphrased the line he used at home plate of Yankee Stadium in 1939. That's the power of a good computer. It lets a guy like me dig up a fact like that.

But I digress.

Today, I consider myself the second unluckiest man at Headstone Haven. Charles W. Tillsbury nailed first prize.

Charlie died Thursday in the parking lot of "Banana Hammocks," one of those clubs where oiled-up men strip off their clothes and allow bachelorette parties to line their waistbands with dollar bills while the "dancers" gyrate their pelvises to 70's disco music. Banana Hammocks is like Xquisite, that club in the *Magic Mike* movie, only with flabbier abs.

Shortly after closing, the club's bouncer found Charlie behind the wheel of his Range Rover. He didn't spend his last few minutes chasing trends, snorting Fentanyl, or some such. Instead, Charlie died old school with a line of Colombian blow across the dashboard and a syringe in his arm that tested positive for heroin. His heart, unable to decide whether to speed up or to slow down, simply elected to stop right there in the parking lot. For obvious reasons, Banana Hammocks does not have a video camera system monitoring the parking lot. But I could guess that Charlie had been in a hurry to party. The plastic tiara he wore sat at a jaunty angle upon his expensive banker's haircut. He tied his arm off with his Hermes tie and pushed the needle right through the sleeve of his Tom Ford shirt. I got the details straight from the police report.

Like I said, Charles W. Tillsbury coffin-nailed first prize.

I got assigned the job of making Tillsbury's death sound elegiac.

The second unluckiest man at Headstone Haven.

Headstone Haven is the nation's fourth-largest producer of grave markers. We carry a comprehensive catalog of monuments, available in metal, natural stone, and synthetic materials. Our sophisticated engraving software can carve religious symbols, sporting scenes, or portraits. The deceased's passions may be displayed for eternity.

A while back, the surviving relatives of Jimmy Benton, a landscaper from Pineview, Texas, contracted with Headstone Haven. Jimmy, tragically, shuffled off this mortal coil when he slipped and fell into his woodchipper at a job site. His sisters and brother decided upon a simple but elegant red granite monument to commemorate their departed Jimmy.

Headstone Haven happily prepared the marker to their modest specifications and promptly shipped the stone in time for the family funeral at the Restland Cemetery. Every member of Jimmy's high school graduating class, not currently incarcerated, turned up for the funeral. All in attendance sang *Amazing Grace* and watched as the marker was revealed.

Looking back, most attendees agreed that it was Alison Smithson, voted "Snarkiest Senior" by the Pineview graduating class, who first snort-laughed when the linen shroud was ceremoniously removed from the headstone. Quick-witted Alison found post-mortem humor that a man who died in a woodchipper would be remembered with the epitaph, "Rest in Piece." The rest of graduating class and even Reverend Benjamin J. Feelberry of the Loaves and Fishes, Greater Covenant Independent Baptist Church, quickly followed suit.

Headstone Haven settled the subsequent lawsuit brought by the surviving family of Jimmy Benton for an undisclosed amount. The trade journals noted, however, that prior to the legal proceedings, Headstone Haven had been the nation's third-largest producer of grave markers.

But I digress.

A few changes in procedures occurred at the corporate offices following what became known as "The Whopper with the Chopper."

Headstone Haven Headquarters, Triple H as it's known inside the main office, dropped an online job posting seeking an English major with first-rate proofreading skills. They got positively giddy when they received my resume showing that not only did I have a Master's in English composition, but also had edited the college newspaper. They offered me the job after the first interview.

As part of the settlement, they also agreed to buy a first-rate computer for the newly created Director of Quality Control—me. Moon landings had been conducted with less computing capacity than I employed to spell check headstones. The computer also helped translate foreign languages—Gaelic and Latin proved to be the most popular for headstones. Accidentally dropping a line suggesting the deceased was a pedophile (*puer amans*) rather than his wife's true love (*amor purus*) could easily drop us to fifth on the list of grave marker producers.

Thoth does the bulk of the work. That's the name I'd given the computer. In the Egyptian Book of the Dead, Thoth, the ibis-headed deity, performed the role of bookkeeper for the gods. He recorded whether someone moved along in the afterlife. When I explained all this to management at Triple H on the day they unpacked my computer, the suits all nodded their heads. They knew they'd hired the right guy for the job. I nodded back. Two minutes with a search engine had provided me with job security.

My procedure became straightforward. I'd download the proposed text into Thoth and a squiggly blue line appeared under any suspect word. If necessary, I'd do a little research to see if the family wanted the epitaph to read, "Beloved Husband and Fodder," or whether they intended the more traditional inscription. Close calls got kicked up the corporate ladder. Courtney Chernbomb, my boss, signed off on anything that might prove litigious.

As you might imagine, copyediting headstones didn't take a full day, not even at the nation's fourth-largest producer of grave markers. I used my free time and my badass computer to seriously improve my online gaming. I progressed to grandmaster in StarCraft.

But I digress.

One day, Courtney "the Cherminator" hit on a new idea. She shot a memo up the corporate ladder at Triple H that we offer an obituary writing service. Her bullet points included:

· Master's degree in English on staff.

· Excess computer capacity currently underutilized.

· Opportunity to grow corporate profits.

I got cc'd on the memo. I declined to point out that I'd needed the RAM to achieve my status as StarCraft grandmaster. I doubt it would have mattered. The Cherminator captured the suits' hearts with the last bullet point. Dreams of recovering the three-spot danced in their heads. She even whipped up the marketing slogan to go with the new campaign—"Better than they were in Life."

As the proofreader-in-charge, I emailed her that the L in "life" didn't require capitalization. The Cherminator told me that it did. I replied, helpfully, that if the thematic words were capitalized, the T in "they" needed to be uppercase. She answered that the text as written helped audiences distinguish their departed loved one, who certainly was not better in death, from the anonymous and lower-cased "they." She told me to stay in my lane and reminded me that I had been hired for copyediting and not marketing.

I did not reply.

I had to concede that the Cherminator's suggestion proved far superior to Phil Billingsley's idea. Billingsley, vice president for sales, once recommended that Triple H increase market share by engraving objets d' art. He snagged buy-in at the highest levels. I thought that the apostrophe had a great deal to do with the idea's success. Triple H's corporate culture wasn't prepared for a flying comma. The suits called it a paradigm shift in punctuation. His PowerPoint presentations popped.

When Triple H succeeded with a line of personalized birdbaths, Billingsley's upward trajectory seemed limitless. Then a religious blogger complained about the St. Francis of Assisi statue at the Texarkana Nature Center. Holding a dove of peace in his left hand, St. Frank pointed thoughtfully onward with his right. The blogger considered the word "restrooms" beneath his outstretched other hand disrespectful to one of the rock stars of the faith. It became a *cause célèbre* throughout the Texarkana diocese.

Unfortunately for Billingsley, *cause célèbre* had two flying commas. Even the best PowerPoint couldn't overcome a heavy hitter like that.

The last time I checked LinkedIn, Billingsley worked as finance manager at a used car lot in Odessa. Inflatable tube men do not make many punctuation demands.

But I digress.

Although the obituary gig interfered with my StarCraft time, the company did foot the bill for me to download a video from the crack team of obit writers at the *New York Times* and to buy a copy of Pericles' Funeral Oration as well as a couple of anthologies of history's great eulogies and obits. I dipped into those as needed. With Thoth's voice recognition software, I didn't even have to type. I'd dictate a few passages into the computer, and I'd be set. Grieving families got a little misty to learn that I modeled their mom's obit on the style of Lady Diana Spenser's or that Dad's remarks were loosely based on Bob Costas's eulogy for Mickey Mantle. I'd always be careful to use the word "loosely" because the deceased rarely would have won seven World Series titles or have been inducted into the Baseball Hall of Fame like the Mick.

Chernbomb's slogan snagged the attention of the wife of the recently deceased Charles W. Tillsbury. Apparently, gossip about the circumstances of Tillsbury's passing had begun to seep through the hierarchy of Vision Bank, where Charles W. had been known as a strait-laced vice president. The Widow Tillsbury hoped that a bit of pre-emptive spin might help stem the malicious poison that a few disgruntled former co-workers were spreading. She didn't want word to reach Sarah Jones, the branch manager. The Widow Tillsbury paid cash for the complete bereavement package: obituary, social media post, and memorial website design.

As an aside, I couldn't help but notice that the black dress Kate Tillsbury wore to the office highlighted her righteous gams.

As I watched those toned legs leave the Triple H, the Cherminator appeared outside my cubicle. "Don't screw this up."

Looking up into her toilet-water-colored eyes, I assured her that I had no intention to screw anything around here.

Seemingly satisfied, she looked around and then dropped her voice to a conspiratorial whisper. "I've got a friend over at Vision Bank. Their company provides a term life insurance benefit to its executives. The insurance, however, has a turpitude clause. A breach would interfere with Widow Tillsbury's payout. She needs the details buried, at least until she receives the insurance proceeds. Then the company will have to decide whether they want to sue a grieving widow."

I nodded.

"So bring a thought shower down on this one and give it 110%," the Cherminator said.

I think I nodded. Mostly I wondered when I'd fallen asleep and awakened in a Dilbert cartoon.

After she left, I set to work on a rough draft. I listed out the problems to overcome.

· Died at a male strip club parking lot.

· With heroin and cocaine.

· Ruined an expensive shirt.

I felt I could work around the last one. The others snagged me. I frontloaded all the vital statistics, birthdate, death date, survivors, hoping the audience's eyes might glaze over and skim over the salacious stuff. I described how Charlie had been a dedicated manager at the bank, responsible for compliance and audit. Thoth wrote my yawn down as a series of hhhs. I briefly mentioned that Charlie had been supporting local entrepreneurs and had spent his final hours visiting and working with troubled youths. Reading it over, I conceded that it felt a little slapdash—not my best thought shower.

I called the duty sergeant over at the police department. A while back, a disgruntled former employee of Headstone Haven, angry about his pending driving while intoxicated charge had programed the headstone etcher to inscribe the epitaph, "Black and Blue" on a brother officer's marker instead of the preferred choice, "Back the Blue." I'd caught the error before production. My attention to detail had earned me a couple of friends in the local constabulary. They generally repaid the kindness by overlooking when my inattention to detail failed to notice speed limits or stop signs. I explained my dilemma to the sergeant, and he agreed to email a few preliminary investigation notes my way. In exchange, I promised to run the next departmental retirement flyer through Thoth and tidy it up before it got taped to all the elevators at the PD.

"Plenty of heroin in the fellow," the sergeant said as he hit send. "Keeled over before he made it to the booger sugar."

"Only one illegal pharmaceutical. That'll be a great comfort to the widow," I said. "Tell me anything else about the car?"

"Didn't look too hard. Clear case of overdose."

Reports in hand, I drove over to Banana Hammocks. I timed my arrival to coincide with the start of John "Black Jack" Cutler's workday. The police identified Mr. Cutler as the on-site security who found Charlie. I hoped that our conversation might add a human element to my obituary.

A man wearing a leather vest, blue jeans, Doc Martens, and sporting a skull and snakes tattoo on his bicep eyed me as I approached. Maybe I gave off a process server vibe. We worked through it, turned out that John is a StarCraft fan. He envied my grandmaster status. He preferred to be called John; he thought it emphasized his cerebral side. He and his Siamese cat liked to co-write poetry when he wasn't throwing malcontents off the main stage at Banana Hammocks.

He showed me where he found Charlie.

As we walked, I felt my phone vibrate. I ignored the call. John had a cat to feed. He showed me the spot.

I pointed. "This is actually the parking lot of The Hungry Armadillo."

John shook his head. "Lots of our customers use it. They don't want some divorce attorney snapping pictures of their car in our lot. They think using a space designated for a family restaurant gives them anonymity."

"But still, it might mean …" I began, but John shook me off.

"Statistically, our clientele is more apt to be dropping coke and smack than your average Armadillo customer. They're more the cheese fries set."

I didn't argue. My analysis had failed the Which-Goes-Better-With-Ranch-Dressing test. "Find anything else?"

John shook his head. "Usual trash in the parking lot. A couple of cheesy sashes and tiaras dropped by some drunk brides-to-be. Another idiot put a couple of to-go orders on the roof of the car, forgot them, and drove off. Dropped right there in the parking lot." He pointed to a spot about two car lengths behind where we stood.

We shook hands. "May your scratching post always be the most," John said.

Iambic pentameter, I thought. That passes for positively Shakespearian in Siamese/Human poetry collaborations.

Leaving Banana Hammocks, I swung by Vision Bank's main office. I thought maybe I might hear a few kind words about Charlie, maybe I'd see black crepe hung over the customer service window. These are the sorts of heartwarming anecdotes I could work with.

My search ended as quickly as it began. I spied Courtney Chernbomb in one of the offices. She appeared to be making a deposit while on her lunch break. I didn't want to discuss my progress or lack thereof with her. I spun around and hastily exited.

I called the sergeant back and asked for permission to view Charlie's car. He hesitated. Allowing civilians to wander around the auto pound stretched the limits of our agreement. It also risked a felony charge of tampering with evidence.

"You're wasting your time," he said.

"But it's my time."

"Did I mention the confession?" he said.

"Uh, no."

"The forensics guys found your man's cell phone under the seat. They took it to the lab. He recorded a memo to himself."

I heard some pages turning.

"Here it is. He said, 'share a line' and then a bit later, 'bad trip off.' Sounds pretty conclusive from where I sit."

"Share a line? That means another person was in the car. Have you found them?"

The sergeant grunted.

"And bad trip off? Who says trip off? That doesn't make sense."

"He was a novice drug user. Hadn't spent enough time to learn the lingo."

"He could've just done a computer search for the Urban Dictionary. Would've taught him the basics."

"Maybe they got a computer skills class in the next life," the sergeant said.

"So you're saying he went to Hell?"

We moved on from the big philosophical questions surrounding Charlie's afterlife to the negotiation. The sergeant and I cut a deal. He'd let me see the car. I agreed to edit two more documents of his choice. He told me I had to come straight there, shift change would allow me to get in and out of the pound without him having to explain or me getting arrested. I ignored the messages piling up on my phone and beat it over there.

I hoped maybe Charlie had been picking up food for the food bank or maybe I'd find the SUV full of Narcan, the opioid remedy drug. I envisioned a moving paragraph outlining his drug outreach and describing the whole overdose episode as quality control gone awry. I didn't find anything to support my story.

I found a few bits of paper sprinkled like snow on his WeatherTech floor mat. The scraps looked like pieces of a spreadsheet, but I've got an M.A. in English so I could have been wrong.

After the pound visit, I sat in my car thinking about the messages. "Share a line."

Great, I thought, that'll help sell the food bank theory. Perhaps he invited people to write more letters and practice their cursive.

"Bad trip off."

Entrepreneurial dreams about a vacation review website might explain it.

Perhaps not.

I stopped by a coffee shop. I don't know the real name. I call it Coffee Swine. The sign out front advertises coffee &wine. They didn't get the spacing quite right. Every time I looked at it, I saw coffee swine. The owner could have used a proofreader. I ordered a dark roast with a twist of bacon. They just looked at me like I'd suffered a head injury.

But I digress.

I think I'm putting off talking about the next part.

I was sitting at a corner table sipping on my cappuccino when I felt my phone buzzing. I looked. The number of missed messages was positively staggering. I hit 'play.' The Cherminator's voice sounded like she gargled with acid and broken glass just before dialing. She told me that if I wasn't back in the office in five minutes, I was so totally fired.

The message came in eight minutes ago.

I finished my cappuccino. I mean, why not?

The Cherm and a security guard stood at the employee entrance to Triple H when I arrived.

"Totally fired," she repeated. I saw the same glint in her eye as she had when she broke the news to Billingsley.

"Totally fired?" I repeated. "Are you like totally trying to sound like you're totally fifteen?" Having a terminal diagnosis does allow one a certain freedom.

She ignored the shot. Then her face turned sour. "The president says you can quit or be terminated. You've got five minutes to get me a resignation letter."

"What'd I do?"

She snorted. "What did you do? Fat finger error. You published your obit notes. Died at a strip club ... cocaine and heroin ... The lawyer for Tillsbury's widow has already called. The money they're demanding may drop us to number six on the headstone list." She glanced at her phone. "Your five minutes start now."

Security escorted me to my office. While Thoth booted up, I collected my few personal possessions. I slipped Pericles Funeral Oration into my box. I considered it my severance package.

I sat down at my desk, stunned by the news. My hands shook. I couldn't settle them on the keyboard.

Security looked at his phone. "Tick-tock," he said.

Clearly, they'd sent me the loquacious one.

I switched Thoth to voice-to-text. My voice struggled with the words. "I resign from Headstone Haven effective immediately." I briefly considered adding a meaty quote, perhaps Shakespeare's, 'Judge, O you gods, how dearly Caesar loved him! This was the most unkindest cut of all.' I decided to let it go. This seemed like the place for a short declarative sentence.

I hit print. Thoth spat out my final correspondence. I got a little dewy-eyed thinking about separating from my computer. I thought Thoth did too. I read Thoth's final message.

"I realign from Hearthstone Heaven effecting media tree."

"Tick-tock," security said.

I couldn't help but smile at the message. Voice-to-text was never Thoth's strong suit. Hearthstone was one of my backup online games. Thoth and I've had spent many hours immersed in it. That's what Thoth heard instead of Headstone. It became Thoth's default. It seemed that we'd played more than I realized. I remembered some of the great minion battles we had witnessed together.

But I digress.

Tick tock.

And then I had one of those Road to Damascus moments. That's New Testament language; obit writers learn that stuff. I am also fluent in the Hebrew Bible and the Koran, the other religious texts I have to search. But the point was that I got this sudden flash of insight. Before the security guy could say 'tick-tock,' I snatched up the letter and marched down the office. The Cherminator stood at her office door with her hand outstretched. I pushed past her.

"I'm not resigning to you," I said and barreled straight into the president's office.

He looked surprised when the office door flung open. If I had knocked, he'd likely had time to move his small bong off the desk into a drawer. Of course, if he had, he might have caught Headstone Haven on fire. This might be the second time today that I've saved this place.

"I did not give him permission to barge …" the Cherminator said.

The boss waved her off. "My door is always open."

Not exactly true, but who was I to argue. I considered telling him that I understood about the weed. We'd both had bad days. But instead, I pushed the note in front of him.

He blinked and tried to focus.

"Tillsbury didn't admit to using heroin," I said.

"Wha-what," he mumbled.

"Exactly," I said. "The cops expected to hear a message from a man who overdosed. They heard 'share a line' and 'bad trip off.' He said, 'Sarah lied' and 'bank rip-off.' Of course, he said it after someone had injected him with heroin, so his words sounded like a stoner." I glanced at the pipe for emphasis.

The boss seemed to understand how drugs might make someone wordle their stumbs.

"Sarah is the manager at Vision Bank. Tillsbury oversaw internal audits. He had the proof in hand. I think he met Sarah outside the Hungry Armadillo to lay it out for her. Arranged a private meeting. Give her the chance to resign. He even picked up dinner for him and his wife. The security guard found the containers spilled behind the car. Charlie was too dead to keep his foot on the brake. The vehicle rolled forward down the slight grade in the parking lot."

"Preposterous," the Cherm said. "He just wants to avoid getting fired."

"We see and hear what we expect," I said. "That's how mistakes like Rest in Piece get made."

The boss frowned. He wasn't too stoned to remember that incident.

"Sarah didn't act alone. I think an accomplice helped overpower him and then jam a syringe loaded with heroin into his arm. No junkie shoots themselves through their shirt. The two of them ripped the evidence from his hand. The tie, cocaine, and tiara were just cruel embellishments. If Sarah told Kate Tillsbury the term life had been voided, she and her accomplice could pocket that money too."

"He's the one who posted Tillsbury's information," the Cherminator said.

"I didn't get to be a StarCraft grandmaster by being sloppy with my keystrokes. I didn't accidentally post anything. Thoth can tell us who logged in." I paused and pointed dramatically toward the Courtney Chernbomb. "And we all know who it will be."

"You can't prove anything," she said.

She was right. I had virtually no evidence to back up what I'd said. But the boss was baked so he didn't drill down too deeply into my statements.

"I don't," I said, "but the police will. When they dust the tiara, they'll find the fingerprint of the person who applied that *coup de grâce* to Charles Tillsbury."

The circumflex above the 'a' in *coup de grâce* carried the day. The boss may have been stoned but he still liked flying punctuation. He ordered security to detain Courtney while he called the police. I gave him the direct line to the sergeant.

The police found the fingerprint. Courtney couldn't implicate Sarah fast enough. I talked to the police and stalled until the boss had come down from his weed and hidden the bong. Headstone Haven caught some positive press for solving a murder. The publicity helped us snag some more market share. The sergeant got a commendation for cracking the unsolved murder case. I edited his certificate to perfection. My new boss, Billingsley, let me know that he'd turn a blind eye to my StarCraft gaming on company time.

Kate Tillsbury came by Headstone Haven to thank me personally for solving the murder. Vision Bank paid the full benefit of the term life insurance. She offered to buy me dinner with the proceeds. I'll add that her gams look great even when she's not wearing a black dress.

But I digress.

MURDER FOR SALE

Hunter Liguore

The phone call from my realtor, Dotty Sayer, this morning was unexpected, especially when she told me our dream home had just come available. I grew a little excited, but not much, having had similar calls over the last two years in search of the perfect home.

"No, Obert, this is *your* home—it hits *everything* on your wish list."

Listening, I nodded as she went through some of the salient features: three bedrooms; two full baths; a sun porch; a kitchen nook leading to a deck; central air; nice yard; low taxes.

"Sounds too good to be true," I said, calling my wife Alandra over, putting the call on speaker so we could both hear. "What's the catch?"

"No catch. You can look at it—well, *now;* there's no wait. Early worm gets the apple."

We drove together across town to 2411 Wistable Terrace, still in sweatpants and t-shirts after our morning workout, with cold brew coffee in to-go mugs in tow. Alandra tried to bring up photos of the listing on her cellphone, unsuccessfully. We grew worried, but then got a text from Dotty saying she was already there and waiting for us, allowing us to write it off as being *too new*. With twenty minutes to go, we allowed ourselves to dream some.

"We can put our workout room in the sunroom ..." began Alandra, smiling, sketching where things might go on the back of an old receipt.

"... and with three bedrooms, one can be just for your crafts ... maybe it will overlook a pretty view for inspiration."

"Oh, a whole room—I won't have to box everything up every time I make a new wreath!"

Even though we dreamed, we took a moment to appreciate our twenty-year-old home that had been *really* good to us. We said things like, *we got lucky,* or *it's not that we need more or better,* it would just be nice to have *less,* something small so we could nestle into retirement like two old birds in five years, with less visibility of neighbors and stores, less noise, and more simplicity and quiet.

"Should we name it, our possible new house?" Alandra asked, jotting down a few ideas.

"It's tradition!" I reminded. "The house is on Wistable Terrace, which sounds like a cozy neighborhood that's always sleeping ... how about, *Sleepy Wishing Well Home*?"

She gave a small peep of appreciation. "Or how about Obertlandra Wishes Come True Homestead."

"Not bad," I said, adding, "I like where you're going with it." We laugh and keep dreaming what it might be like to *actually* sleep in a new place, with new views, and possibly all the things we wanted in a house.

My wife gave a sigh. "I just want to one day be able to say, 'the search is over,' and we're home."

"Me too, babe. Me too." I take her hand and we start reminiscing about the dreadful houses we'd been led to, by several realtors, before signing with Dotty a few weeks ago—like the Mold House, that was green on the outside—*and inside* ... the radiators had blown, spraying the ceiling and walls and then left sealed up, turning it a nice turquoise blue *everywhere.* "I gotta guy," the realtor at the time had said. "He can fix this for a couple-o-hundred bucks, no problem." Try thousands. Next, please!

"Or the dungeon house ..." She mimicked the next congenial agent. "... and here, in the basement, your very own dungeon to hide a corpse!" She recapped the details of the two-by-ten stone room behind a rugged, locked door with metal hooks, hidden in the corner of the basement.

"*Brrr* ... gives me a chill and the shivers."

"Oh! Remember the one with the pet cemetery on the front lawn?"

I laughed. "That was something else! I didn't know they made headstones so small."

Dotty had come highly recommended from our friends Jean and Tommy, who said it only took two weeks to get their dream house. "You give her your list," Jean said. "And *presto,*" Tommy added, "she finds it a few days later!"

With a 100% success rate, and a 5-star rating on HomeyFinder.com, we figured we had nothing to lose.

Pulling onto Wistable Terrace, we were both excited: met with a neighborhood of pretty lawns and cute eco-ranches, we started to *ooh* and *ahh* the cozy sidewalks, the plentiful flower gardens and bird feeders, not to mention the quiet. Nowhere did we see the Two-of-Everything Offenders, the kind of people who had two cars and two extra cars for good measure; but also a trailer for vacations and another just 'cause; a pool above and below; a big shed and a little shed … and lawn furniture and a flock of flamingoes—a caboose, on one occasion—covering every inch of the yard—sometimes the roof and their neighbors' yards too …

"Looks nice …" I took Alandra's hand, assuredly.

"So far," she said, afraid, it seemed, to hope.

"Let's just go and see it. We don't have to make *any* decisions today."

"Okay. But if it's not listed, we might be first, and might actually win the bid fairly. So we should hurry."

"Yeah, that's one way." I told her. "Let's take *our* time." I knew how the game was played: we'd get a measly fifteen minutes to see what might be our home for the next twenty years, rushed through so fast it'd leave us nauseous, and then we'd be pressed to make a bid on the spot, usually for ten to fifty thousand dollars more than the asking price, to be *competitive*, like we're athletes suddenly. "We'll do what's right for us and go from there."

"Okay. But what if we *really* like it."

"We'll go crazy and buy the darn thing, okay, my love."

Alandra softens, squeezing my hand.

As the car came to a full-stop, we were both silent.

"Um … what …"

I tried to see around the police task force and forensic team setting up on the lawn of 2411 Wistable Terrace.

"What was the address?" I finished. "It can't be that one."

"What do you think happened?" Alandra asked, slowly getting out of the car.

"I'll ask." I got out, noticing an elderly woman gripping her small dog on her doorstep, watching the commotion. "Hi there. What's going on?"

"Murder," she said, looking me up and down, as the dog barked, and then went inside hurriedly.

I looked at Alandra. She looked at me. She spoke first, checking her cellphone. "We probably have the street wrong."

"Got to be."

"Obert! Alandra! Over here!" Dotty was waving at us from the front of 2411, the police tape caught around her ankle, as she came to greet us.

"You're here, finally!" She gave us a jovial group hug. "Well, what did I tell you, *DREAM HOME!*" Her tone was singsong. "We don't have a second to lose—look! They're lining up as we speak!" She pointed to another group of cars, with another couple gaping like us, about to be pressed on by their realtor. "There's no way they're getting in there before us! Let's go!"

"GO? Go where?"

"Oh, here, you'll need to wear these plastic booties on your feet."

Surprisingly, we did as she asked, and followed her into the house, sidestepping our way past the vast array of uniformed workers.

"Now over here is the living room," began Dotty. "Just avert your eyes at the obvious. We can probably ask for a new rug allowance—in all the rooms, by the look of it." She pointed to the red footprints staining the tan carpet down the hallway.

"Are we allowed to be in here?" Alandra asked, squeezing closer to me.

"Yeah, I mean, the blood doesn't even look dry." No sooner had I said it, had a drop of the cherry red stuff dripped off the ceiling onto the couch.

"CCTV, Lovelies, we had it checked this morning, clearing both of you. And their not too worried: tamper with the evidence and you'll never get a closing date, am I right!" She opened the door on the fireplace. "What do you think? Picture the romantic dinners you can have in here—a little picnic, just the two of you, roasting marshmallows, cracking open a bottle of wine."

Alandra jabbed me with her elbow. "Is that ... *is that*?"

I saw it too, the bloodied fire poker wrapped in plastic. I pointed to it. Dotty showed surprise at first, then heaved a sigh, a bit annoyed. "Don't worry; they'll get to it. Why don't we make our way to the kitchen?"

Just then, the other realtor and couple appeared in the foyer, beginning their house tour, kicking off my competitive edge. "The audacity," I whispered to Alandra. "I can't believe they aren't even going to give us our *fifteen* minutes!"

"They won't rush me," she said, crossing her arms, looking at her watch. "I'm taking my time." She started asking Dotty some questions. "How old are the appliances?"

"Let's see here." She had her tablet out, scrolling. "Luckily, they're stainless steel or it'd be a real bungle to clean up ... oh, looks like they just upgraded. It's all brand new, even the floor."

With the body of the husband, lying face down in front of the fridge, it made it impossible to get a real sense of how big the room was—but then, he was in pieces, so it kinda offered us an imaginary view of what it would be like with multiple people—or at least, that's how Dotty sold it to us. Add the sliding doors that led to a private deck, we were starting to see the potential.

Alandra gave a sharp gasp! "Oh, Obert! Quickly!"

I found her in the sunroom, blood pooled at her feet. "What is it?"

"Picture the treadmill here," she said, pointing to the kneeling forensic tech, scrutinizing the husband's severed head.

The forensic tech looked up, pointing to the corner. "You'll have a better view if you put it there."

"Oh, you're right!" Alandra lit up. "Weights in the corner, yeah?"

"And it's all central air," Dotty added, as if on cue. "And voila! You have your own gym."

I nearly slipped crossing the room, still getting used to the plastic booties. "We'll name it, *Obertlandra Fit*. We can even get a sign."

"Repaint the wall," said the forensic tech, "and hang it there; it'll look real nice."

"I agree," said Alandra, her smile disappearing when the other couple and realtor encroached.

"Don't let them get to you," I said. "We're still ahead of them by a few minutes." With things looking good so far, I began calculating what we could afford to offer, minus moving costs … "Hey, Dotty," I asked, as we made our way to the bedrooms. "They'll get a cleaning crew in here, right?"

"Already here, Love. With the house shortage looming, as soon as forensics gets what they need, the cleaners get 'a vacuuming. But don't you worry, I'm sure we can get new paint and maybe hardwood floors throughout … What do you say about that?"

"Sounds perfect!" Alandra said, smiling, squeezing my hand, whispering. "This could be it … I mean, it's a little crowded, and well, you know, the smell is like …"

"Rank laundry? Yeah, I noticed that too."

Dotty, overhearing, told us it would air out quickly. "It'll smell like a new car in here when they're done."

The first bedroom was remarkably tidy, a nice place for storage, we concluded. The next one, despite the bullet holes through the closet doors, had potential to be a decent craft room.

I went to the window and opened the curtains to see the view. Past the tipped chair, with grandma cut in two, was a pretty flower garden.

Dotty spoke up. "Those graves the police are digging up, false alarms, turns out they got a bad tip that there were more bodies hidden out there—and too bad, we might've been able to negotiate off the list price if they had."

"And the master bedroom?" I asked.

"Let's see if we can get in there." Dotty waved us on. "It'll be crowded, but you can get the gist of how big it is—the walk-in closet's to die for."

Once we managed to get inside the room, we watched a few minutes while the forensic team scraped up the soft brain, or flecks of skin, and a few toes, putting them in jars. The bathroom was off limit, as it seemed the wife had been cut into little pieces and flushed—or tried to, Dotty explained, like she had the story first-hand.

"Could be bad for the plumbing," she explained. "But we can work around it—we'll make your offer contingent on a full septic and pipe inspection; obviously, we'll get someone over here to pump it out, soon as we can. But the size of the room has lots of space—you can mount a screen on this wall and presto! Instant home theater, am I right?"

"The house is just the right size for us," I said, looking around. "Is there a basement?"

"No," said Dotty. "Slab for storage … they have the dogs searching it, so we'll have to wait on that." She scrolled on her tablet. "Looks like this lot was only the second family to live here. Seems like they took good care of it, wouldn't you say?"

"Any leads on … you know, who's responsible?"

"Between the task force you see here and the amateur detectives online already following the story, it won't be long before they have a suspect. Would it be a deal-breaker if the murderer was at-large?"

We thought about it, deliberating. I said, "I think we'd kind of like to know that the neighborhood was safe, that there wouldn't be a repeat, you know, next door, or down the block, since the whole point of moving was less people and more quiet."

"I hear your concern," said Dotty. "I'm sure by the time we go to closing …"

"How soon? Is it three months now?"

"Oh, no, the whole process is done in a few days … streamlined now, with so many houses selling every day. But you better make a decision quick, as it looks like this couple might steal it out from under you!"

The other couple were clearly making calculations on their cellphone, deliberating. I heard the wife say, "I want this house," causing me to turn to Alandra, and ask the most important question. "Is this *our* house?"

"Can I look at the living room again?"

"Certainly," said Dotty. "We haven't even been here a full fifteen minutes."

We had to wait as one of the bodies was carted out in a morgue bag, but it gave us more time to check out things like the lighting and heating system; we also started seeing if there were any goodies we might want to keep with the house—like they had a couple of retro video game consoles I had my eye on; Alandra spotted an old sewing machine and fabric.

"I'll do my best," Dotty said, sure she could get them for us if our bid was accepted.

In the living room, Alandra laid out a piece of plastic on the furniture and sat, trying to imagine what it would be like if it were our home. She was saying something, pointing to the fireplace, but I couldn't hear over the ambulance pulling away.

"Lovelies, I don't want to spoil the fun, but there is another group coming in, and several more lining up. This other couple looks like they're making a bid—if you want it, you're going to have to decide and give me a figure."

I took Alandra's hands into mine, reminding her we always wanted a house with a sunroom and deck. "It really is perfect."

"I say, let's do it!" Alandra hugged me around the neck, then kissed me. "We want it! This is our home!"

"Excuse us, please," said the officer, "we're looking for a missing finger—have you seen it?"

Dotty was quick to find it near the fireplace, and stepped aside, ushering us along. "No point in delaying—I've got the paperwork ready to go. You just need to tell me your price and sign."

With the next family coming into the already crowded space, we decided to go outside to finish things. I took one last look around, imagining what it'd be like to live there. As much as I really liked the place, something felt *off*. I just couldn't put a finger on it, though I didn't let on, not wanting to disappoint Alandra, who seemed really in love with the place.

Outside, the police put up more tape along the driveway as a means to crowd-control the growing number of realtors and clients there to see the house.

Underneath the catalpa tree, we held our fingers out to sign the bid. Alandra went first, starting the A, then stopped, looking at me.

"I know that look. What's wrong with the house?"

Dotty gave a chuckle. "It's just nerves. Go on, sign it. We haven't much time. We want our offer to be first and strong ... they're not going to want to sit on this one."

Alandra nervously chuckled, agreeing. "Twenty years in one house—it's time, right?" She went to sign again and stopped, glancing at me again. She had the same look on our first date, when I showed up on her doorstep with a carton of almond milk and toilet paper—two items I'd mistakenly thought she'd mentioned needing—and even though I was *way off*, she found me adorable for trying to be considerate and thoughtful. This time, I knew it was the look that said she didn't need a new home, so much as she enjoyed dreaming about our future, together.

On the car ride home, we were quiet, as it took time to get to the end of the street with the media trucks rolling in to cover the story.

"Gosh, they're late to the party."

"No kidding," she said, glancing back through the back window.

"So what was it," I asked, "the deal-breaker?"

"You should know."

At the same time, we both said it, "The fireplace!"

We cracked up, laughing.

Incredulous, I said, "Why would anybody want a fireplace in this day and age!"

"I know!" Alandra said, "And all the realtors think it's a selling point—"

"And NONE OF THEM will tell you all it's going to do it suck the heat out of your house in the winter."

We laughed some more, lacing our hands together.

"The sunroom was nice," I said.

"But it's probably as hot as a greenhouse in the summer, even with central air."

"Good point." She started texting.

"Is that to Jean and Tommy, letting them know their superstar agent wasn't so super?"

"It's to the police," she said, matter-of-factly, tilting the phone to show me a photo; I couldn't make out the details while driving.

I shook my head, confused. "What is it?"

"It's the poker."

"So."

"So? It happens to have casually gone from the fireplace to Dotty's car—I think she was trying to hide it."

"Hmm, interesting—and she *was* a little too aggressive with us when we said we didn't want the house, like it was personal."

"Not the craziest way to get a listing." Alandra sent the text. "Remember the realtor who showed us the house and the people were still living in it ..."

"They were having a barbeque on the patio, if I remember correctly."

We laughed.

"If she goes to jail, we'll need a new realtor again ..."

"Or ..."

We pulled into our driveway, our twenty-year old house waiting for us. It was a bit worn, but it was ours.

"We're home," Alandra said.

"Yeah, babe, this time, I really think we are."

THE SWEET COUPLE NEXT DOOR

Edward Lodi

It was a mean thing to do. That much I'll admit. When they moved in next-door the Donavons seemed like such a sweet couple: kind, considerate, eager to lend a helping hand. Why would anyone want to harm them?

In the end, though, what choice did I have?

When my long-time neighbor, Mr. Bellotti, died shortly before Thanksgiving, the family homestead went to his daughter, an only child. Unfortunately—for me, and ultimately for the Donavons—she had established herself on the West Coast, clear across the country, and had no desire to move back East. Consequently once the will cleared probate she hired a real estate agent and put the house up for sale.

It didn't remain long on the market. The Donavons, a childless couple in their late fifties, bought the house and moved in around Memorial Day. At first they seemed like a quiet, unassuming pair. Peg Donavon was frumpy, short and plump, with graying hair and a sallow complexion, the poster child for folks who spend too much time indoors watching TV and eating junk food. Joe Donavon was slightly taller than his wife, slightly plumper, slightly grayer, equally dull.

Anyhow, to welcome them to the neighborhood I baked an apple pie and carried it over while it was still warm. Before I had a chance to knock, Peg answered the door.

"I saw you crossing the yard through the window," she explained. "Apple pie! How neighborly! Hubby's favorite."

Just then Hubby appeared at the door wearing a broad grin that revealed more teeth than seemed necessary. I introduced myself.

"Mrs. Fernandes," they chimed in unison. "We're lucky to have such a kind neighbor," Peg added. "Aren't we, Joe?"

Joe nodded vigorously, like one of those novelty bobbing heads some fools place at the rear windows of their cars.

"It's *Miss* Fernandes," I corrected them. "But please, call me Sarah." I won't bore you with details of the idle chatter that followed, other than to say that they invited me in for coffee and to share the pie, but I declined.

"I have to get home and pack. I'm flying out to Maryland tomorrow to visit my sister for two weeks." Sally, caregiver for her invalid husband, was in desperate need of respite, which I'd gladly furnish, but I didn't burden the Donavons with any of that.

"Is there anything we can do while you're away?" Peg Donavon asked eagerly. "Take care of a pet? Water plants?"

"I don't have a pet, or indoor plants in need of care," I replied. "But thanks anyway."

"The least I can do is mow your lawn," Joe insisted.

"No, please. I'd rather you didn't, though it's kind of you to offer." With that I took my leave.

I should have been more adamant.

Two weeks later I returned from Maryland exhausted but gladdened by the knowledge that I'd given my sister a much-needed rest. But when the airport limo pulled up in front of my house the sight that greeted me robbed me of much of that gladness. Someone had mowed the lawn.

That someone had to be Joe Donavon, my new neighbor. After I'd explicitly asked him not to. Of course he had cut the grass much too short, gouging the turf, causing permanent damage, and worse—much worse—he'd mowed the foliage of the daffodils and tulips along the borders. Anyone with half a brain knows that once daffodils and tulips have bloomed you have to let the leaves alone until they wither and turn brown. Cutting them back while they're still green—even worse, *mowing* them—ensures that they won't bloom next year, or the next, and possibly not the year after that. The damn fool!

Well, there was no help for it. The damage was done. Eventually I'd go next door and administer a gentle rebuke. For now, though, the chaise longue out back beckoned. I quickly slipped out of my travel clothes into shorts and a loose-fitting top, fixed a tall gin and tonic, and strolled out the back door onto the patio.

Only to behold even greater destruction.

Those fools. Those troglodytes. Those blathering idiots. They'd laboriously, meticulously, irrevocably, scraped away every speck of moss from the surface of the patio. The moss that bridged the crevices between the patio blocks. The moss whose plush green softened the hard pavers. The living carpet that absorbed heat on even the hottest of days. The moss that supplied nesting material for sparrows, wrens, and humming birds. The moss that took decades to grow. The moss that I would never in my lifetime see restored to its former glory.

But wait—that was only the beginning of the desecration wrought by the Donavons.

At the edge of my property, where grass sloped gently down to merge into wetlands, there had stood a centuries-old oak. Several years ago lightning struck the tree, splitting it in two. As a consequence it was slowly dying. And yet it still provided food and shelter for wildlife. Woodpeckers drilled for insects and their larvae, cavity-nesting birds—chickadees, titmice, nuthatches—raised their young, and high up on the trunk a flying squirrel had its home. Even had the tree died outright I would have left it standing, so beneficial was it to creatures of the wild, so picturesque did it appear on the landscape, so etched was it in my imagination.

In my absence Joe Donavon cut it down.

Not by himself, of course. He must've had help. Joe and his fellow desecrators, whoever they were, had stripped the massive trunk of its limbs, which they'd then cut—and split—into firewood. Then they'd hacked away at the trunk until they were able to topple it. This, too, they cut into fireplace wood. All of it neatly stacked in a corner of the yard where, by happenstance, my septic system lay buried. Hopefully they had not damaged it. In any case, the wood would have to be moved.

Too bad fireplace wood requires at least a year of curing before it's dry enough to burn. For I pictured Joe bound to a stake, with gasoline-soaked wood stacked up to his waist, and me touching off the blaze with a lighted torch. His howls of agony as the flames licked his chin would do little to assuage my rage at the enormity of what he'd done, but they'd be better than nothing.

Rather than indulge myself in further fantasies of vengeance, however, I did what any rational human being would do in similar circumstances and polished off the gin and tonic, without pausing for breath. I then fixed myself another, this one a bit stronger than the first, and drank it in the living room, where I could pretend that nothing had happened during my absence.

Only then did I trust myself to venture next door.

Again, Peg answered my knock before I'd completed it, catching me with fist in mid swing. As we stood facing each other, she with a shit-eating grin on her face, I with my knuckles clenching air, I was tempted to smash those same knuckles into her face.

But being of a practical nature I refrained. The last thing I wanted was a charge of assault and battery brought against me. So instead I lowered my fist and attempted a smile.

"Sarah! Back so soon! How time flies. Did you have a good trip? But where are my manners? Come in. I'll put on a pot of coffee and you can tell Joe and me all about Maryland."

Like a dog hearing its name, Joe materialized behind his wife. Judging by the insipid grin on his face, I sensed that he expected words of gratitude to gush through my lips.

Happy to disappoint, I treated him to gall. "Joe, I distinctly remember asking you not to mow my lawn."

"Oh, it was nothing, Sarah. We're always happy to help a neighbor, aren't we Peg."

"You don't understand." I went on to explain the damage he'd caused, not only to the lawn, but to the spring bulbs. I then expressed the dismay I felt at the harm he and his cohorts (for he confessed that he and Peg had enlisted the aid of their church group in their "charitable endeavors") had done to the beauty of my back yard, let alone to wildlife. Although Joe and Peg appeared contrite, I think they were more puzzled than sorrowful. Why would anyone want ugly moss growing on their patio? Why would someone not be grateful for the removal a tree that was nothing more than an eyesore?

Before I left I exacted a solemn promise that they would make no further changes to my property, no matter how well intentioned. In hindsight, what I should have said was simply, "Do me a favor: don't do me any favors."

For the next month or so things went well, with three notable exceptions. The first incident occurred one morning when I was weeding the marigolds I'd planted along my side of the stone wall separating my property from the Donavons'. I saw Joe with a stick poking around the stones on his side, doing what, I couldn't imagine, nor did I care, so long as he stayed on his side of the property line.

Suddenly I heard a loud thwack. "Gotcha!" Joe exclaimed. "Third one today," he shouted over to me.

"Third what?" I asked, a sinking sensation in the pit of my stomach.

"Look." Proudly he held up the stick, on the end of which dangled a dead snake.

For years I'd known of the family of ringneck snakes living in the stone wall. Not only were the ringnecks harmless, they were beneficial, devouring insects and slugs.

I fought back my anger. "Those snakes aren't poisonous. They have a right to live."

Joe chuckled. "Peg's terrified of 'em. I promised her I'd kill every last one."

I tried to argue with the moron but he wouldn't listen. "Peg hates anything creepy-crawly," he insisted. "Gotta keep the little lady happy."

After that I tried to avoid my neighbors whenever possible. The extermination of the ringnecks made me sick. I couldn't stomach witnessing any other crimes against nature the two might be perpetrating.

To some, the next "incident" might seem innocuous, nothing to get riled up about. But clearly, no matter how well-intentioned, it was a crime against the environment. One afternoon as I returned home from grocery shopping I happened to glance into the Donavons' back yard. Spade in hand, Joe was planting flowers all along his side of the stone wall. Beautiful deep purple flowers with tall spikes.

"Joe," I hollered. "What are you doing? You can't plant those in your yard."

He looked up, bewildered.

"Those are purple loosestrife," I explained.

"Oh, is that what they're called? They endangered? There's hundreds of 'em growing in the swamp out back. I only dug up a few. Hardly put a dent in 'em."

"They're anything but endangered. Purple loosestrife are highly invasive. Environmentalists spend millions of dollars each year attempting to eradicate them."

"Peg loves 'em," Joe countered. "A few along the wall won't do no harm."

I knew enough not to argue. Nothing I said would dissuade Joe. Already he and Peg viewed me as a quarrelsome old biddy. I did blow my top, however, when a few days later I was awakened at dawn by what sounded like a leaf blower underneath my bedroom window. It turned out to be a crew of three fanning out on the Donavons' property, looking like astronauts in their protective masks and cumbersome suits, spraying a fine mist onto everything in sight. As though that weren't bad enough, the mist was drifting into my yard.

I didn't need to see the logo on the truck parked in the Donavons' driveway to know that the crew were spraying for mosquitoes and ticks. I'm not particularly fond of mosquitoes and ticks, but I do appreciate butterflies, dragonflies, hummingbird moths, bumblebees, and the myriads of other insects the toxic spray would also kill. On *my* property as well as on the Donavons'.

By the time I dressed and stormed next door it was too late. The damage was done. That didn't prevent me from lashing out and giving the Donavons a piece of my mind. During my tirade they looked at me with open-mouthed dismay. If previously they had viewed me as nothing more than a pest, they now saw me as a woman gone mad. I could see the pity in their eyes. Of course, that infuriated me all the more.

After that I gave up. Their stupidity was impenetrable. When, in the fall, they heaped up brush and leaves they'd raked and made a bonfire of it all, I didn't protest, even though the prevailing wind blew the smoke onto my property, and I came down with the worst dose of poison ivy I'd ever suffered, from the smoke of the leaves of the plant they'd unknowingly included in their pile.

Peg must have felt sorry for me, for she appeared at my door one afternoon with a tuna fish casserole she'd baked. "It's my specialty," she assured me. "It's Joe's favorite. I just know you'll love it."

I have to admit the casserole tasted good. I ate it for supper. The trouble was, it gave me food poisoning. It made me violently ill. When Joe learned of this he apologized profusely. "I told Peg she shouldn't of left it on the counter all those hours. I'm not surprised it spoiled. Is there anything we can do to make amends?"

What with the itch from the poison ivy rash and the misery in my gut I merely shook my head, and closed the door in his face.

How much more of this could I bear?

The answer soon came. My brother-in-law took a turn for the worse, and I rushed off to Maryland to assist my sister in any way I could. When the crisis was over I flew back to Massachusetts, fearful of what I might find upon my return. With the Donavons, one never knew.

When I stepped out of the airport limo, the sight that greeted my eyes confirmed my worst fears. The Donavons had been at work. With winter coming on they'd thoughtfully provided me with a supply of fireplace wood, neatly stacked on the farmer's porch attached to the front of my house. It was their way of saying, "Please forgive us."

Too bad. After all, they meant well. But the fireplace wood was the proverbial straw. It sealed their fate.

Cardinal rule of home ownership: DO NOT stack wood next to your house. In particular, DO NOT stack next to your house wood that has lain on the ground for three or four years. Wood that has become infested with insects.

Termites? I should've been so lucky. In the early stages of infestation termites are relatively easy to exterminate. Expensive, but not budget-breaking. So, if not termites, what was the unintended gift the Donavons bestowed upon me?

Powder post beetles.

Powder post beetles merit their name by rendering posts (read all wood) into, you guessed it, powder. Even in the early stages the little buggers (no pun intended) are a nightmare to be rid of. The best method—essentially, the only method—is to wrap your house tightly in plastic and pump in poisonous gas, and say a prayer or two at the same time.

Not all exterminators are capable of doing this. The closest I could find to New England had to fly in from the South. Not cheap.

Gin, on the other hand, is relatively inexpensive. After the exterminators left I headed out to the nearest package store and bought half a dozen bottles. With time to kill before I could safely enter the house, I drove on to The Oak Barrel Tavern and treated myself to a couple of gin martinis. Thus fortified, I returned home and proceeded to get uproariously drunk.

And stayed that way for three solid days.

In the aftermath of the hangover I began to plot my revenge.

When you have a problem with pests you call in the exterminators. Or, you can handle the problem yourself. As an example, take the Donavons. To kill ticks and mosquitoes they called in the professionals. But to rid themselves of snakes, Joe undertook the task. To save my house from powder post beetles I hired experts. To rid myself of the Donavons ... let's just say I felt equal to the task.

Ever since the Donavons moved in next door I've had to take sedatives at night in order to sleep. The first thing I did after recovering from my three-day binge was to refill the prescription, after which I baked an apple pie. Then, putting on my best smile, I carried the pie over to the Donavons.

When Peg answered my knock and saw who it was she stood speechless. The expression of surprise on her face was quickly followed by one of suspicion. "Sarah?"

"Good afternoon, Peg," I beamed. "I see you're surprised to see me." I looked down at my feet, as if abashed. "Look, I know I've been a difficult neighbor. You and Joe have been so nice and, well, I'm afraid I haven't been very nice in return. I've said some rude things." I shrugged. "Anyhow, to say I'm sorry I baked one of my apple pies. I know how much Joe enjoys them."

Accepting the pie, Peg thanked me, but did not invite me in. Just as well. I would have declined the invitation anyhow.

Now all I had to do was wait. Knowing Joe, by evening he would have consumed at least two slices of pie, more likely three or four. Peg would have eaten at least one. Though I make a fantastic apple pie, most of the credit belongs to my grandmother, who handed down to me her own secret recipe. The extra ingredient I added for the Donavons would not, I hoped, alter the taste.

As soon as the sun sank below the horizon I walked over to the Donavons and knocked on the door. Just as I expected, there was no response. The liberal dose of sedative I'd added to the apple pie had taken effect.

The rest was simple. Under cover of darkness I lugged slabs of the firewood Joe and his cohorts had so thoughtfully prepared for me and arranged them in a pile on the front stoop of the Donavons' wood-frame house. Joe kept his shed unlocked, which saved me the trouble of going back to my own shed for the gasoline I needed to ignite the wood. I drenched the pile, struck a match, and slowly made my way back home, where I fixed myself a stiff gin and tonic, and sat by the window in anticipation of the light show.

Those old wood-frame houses go up like tinder boxes. I'm sure Peg and Joe never woke up, never felt a thing. Anyhow I'm not sorry for what I did. Do you think I can plead insanity? After all, the Donavons drove me crazy.

THE GREEN BURGLAR

A You-Solve-It by John H. Dromey

Despite his slight build and his overall cherubic outward appearance, Sydney "Baby Face" Tanner was far from being an angel. Sadly, he became a delinquent at a very early age. Perhaps his genes were at least partly to blame. Both of his parents were career criminals and, consequently, less-than-perfect role models.

Encouraged to follow in his father's footsteps, Syd started out small. Physically, he was ill-equipped to take giant strides on the path to perdition. Instead, he took baby steps as he passed the low-numbered mile markers on the road to ruin.

Growing up in a time before everybody and his pup had a cell phone, Syd got away with all sorts of questionable behavior.

For a few short years, the tiny tyke was a successful playground bully. As a side hustle, he extorted lunch money from his classmates.

In sharp contrast to his rambunctious outdoor escapades during recess, Syd's behavior in the classroom was exemplary. He made good grades and ingratiated himself with his instructors. On occasion, he even attained the status of teacher's pet. That exalted rank buffered him somewhat from the badmouthing of fellow students and their irate parents. As a direct result, Syd's miscreant activities continued unchecked.

Then, something changed. The other kids his age experienced an early growing spurt, especially the girls. As soon as his contemporaries started to look down on him, literally, Syd's bad behavior had to be redirected. That point was driven home, emphatically, when his bluff was called and he lost three fistfights in quick succession.

Rather than take early retirement from a life of delinquency, Syd joined the family business.

The youngster's organized crime debut got off to a rocky start. It was his job to cast the first stone—a chunk of concrete, or a brick—and then to look innocent when the police showed up to investigate the incident. His vandalism was in fact a diversion. Syd was a decoy to keep the police busy while his parents burglarized a jewelry store or some other small business in another part of town.

Any time he was apprehended, Syd claimed there were mitigating circumstances that would surely prohibit law enforcement representatives from concluding he was destructive by nature. He spun fanciful yarns of being tempted on rare occasions to perform acts of civil disobedience, supposedly in response to harrowing episodes of ill-treatment in the past. Sometimes, he drew on his intimate knowledge of misbehavior by schoolyard bullies to make his case. In retelling an embellished version of events, Syd portrayed himself as a perpetual victim. At the same time, he maintained a meek demeanor and slouched down to emphasize his slight stature. More often than not, without requesting someone from Social Services to verify his current family situation, Syd was offered ice cream and a ride home rather than being arrested.

The wayward lad's troubled childhood was followed by an angst-filled adolescence. Although he eventually inched his way up to almost average height, his criminal ambition did not grow apace. His fate was sealed long before his juvenile records were. After carefully weighing his options, Syd picked a profession in which size did not matter. He became a sneak thief.

On his own, at last, Syd continued his chosen career as a criminal. He specialized in residential burglaries. Anyone who left home without locking his doors became an easy target.

Syd's preferred MO for locating houses to rob was cruising high-end neighborhoods in a nondescript vehicle with a detachable pizza delivery sign on the roof. Bogus license plates added an extra layer of protection.

The burglar prided himself on being prepared for any contingency. One afternoon, he was at a 4-way stop with his windows rolled down.

A pedestrian asked, "Where are you headed?"

Syd pointed to an insulated bag on his passenger seat and mentioned a phony address he'd determined in advance of his scouting trip.

"That's one street over," the pedestrian said.

Syd turned in the direction the man pointed. An unremarkable encounter that would soon fade from the observer's memory.

With no unforeseen hiccoughs, it was crooked business as usual for a while.

Then one evening, while the diminutive thief was watching a pirated cable channel on a high-definition, large-screen TV set that had conveniently "fallen off the back of a truck," a documentary came on about saving the planet through reduced energy consumption and the protection of natural resources. Right then and there, Syd had a revelation. He resolved to reform his life. For the first time in a very long time, he took a night off from work. He left his lint-free nylon cat burglar suit in the closet right next to his high-end crepe-soled footwear.

The next day, Syd boosted a bicycle. Two wheels, ten speeds, but no motor. He decided, in future, to confine his criminal activities to nearby neighborhoods. Furthermore, he was determined to steal only currency, antique jewelry, and small, energy-efficient appliances.

Syd paid cash for a perpetual flashlight that converted motion into enough electricity to power the tiny long-lived lightbulb. Next, he visited a thrift shop and outfitted himself in dark clothing, ranging from a tattered-ski-mask-covered head to dilapidated-athletic-shoe-encased toe. His new ensemble was made mostly of natural fibers with the notable exception of the scarred, synthetic-material sneakers.

Syd got lucky on a subsequent late-night outing. Moonlight coming through French windows helped guide him across a cream-colored carpet to a valuable antique wind-up clock perched on top of a high mantelpiece. Since it was a warm evening, the fire was out. Syd wanted the energy-neutral timepiece for his personal use. Because of his short arms, he had to remove the fireplace screen and stand in the firepit in order to reach the loot sitting on the mantel.

After hiding his stolen bicycle in some dense shrubbery, Syd carried the old clock home on shank's mare. He'd return for the bike later.

During the long walk, the Green Burglar wondered if keeping identifiable stolen property in his home was a good idea. He thought, *wouldn't it be ironic if the authorities caught me because of my doing something that's actually worthwhile?* The saying "*no good deed goes unpunished*" briefly crossed his mind, but Syd dismissed the notion out-of-hand. Since he was too careful to get caught, there would be no probable cause for issuing a search warrant for his property.

Continuing to rely on his youthful appearance, Syd developed a fixed routine for fencing his stolen goods. He used public transportation to reach pawn shops located close to a community college. Wearing a backpack, he could easily be mistaken for a commuting student.

A successful summer was followed by a financially-fulfilling fall.

With the arrival of cold weather, Syd made a minor adjustment in his wardrobe. Whenever he went outdoors, whether working or not, he wore his decrepit sneakers. The synthetic material was exponentially warmer than unlined leather footwear.

One winter evening, Syd was out for a leisurely stroll along a well-lit street when he was stopped for a possible curfew violation.

While one of the neighborhood patrol officers checked Syd's ID, her partner turned on his bodycam and examined the fresh tracks the young man's shoes made in the dusting of snow that covered the sidewalk.

"Hey, Lucy!" Officer Cody called out a minute later. "You need to take a gander at these miniature works of art. They're like a cross between a monochromatic crazy quilt and a disjointed Picasso portrait."

Officer Lucy Bishop took a closer look and nodded her head. "I agree with your assessment, Roy. Would you like to do the honors?"

"We can share. I'll cuff him. You can read him his rights."

"What's going on?" Syd asked.

"You're under arrest on suspicion of being a particularly elusive burglar we've been looking for."

"What makes you suspect me?"

Lucy responded, "I suppose you could say your carbon footprint gave you away."

"What do you think you know about my environmental concerns?"

"Let's not get into specific details. I suggest you exercise your right to remain silent for the time being. You can talk to a lawyer after you've been booked."

Charged with multiple counts of residential burglary, Sydney "Baby Face" Tanner opted for a public defender.

"How did the police get on to me?" he wondered.

Solution in next month's issue ...

SOLUTION TO JUNE'S YOU-SOLVE-IT

Burglar's Bungle by Guy Belleranti

Herman. He slipped up when he said, "Perhaps Molly opened the window to let some fresh air into her bedroom last night and forgot to close it." Since Melch, Sprott and Aunt Molly had never mentioned which window was open, Herman couldn't have known it was Molly's bedroom window unless he was the person who opened it.

Herman had made an extra key prior to installing Aunt Molly's locks. He used this key to get inside. When he finished his stealing he opened the window and pushed out the screen so it would look like the point of entry.